Wit in Love

Wit in Love

by

Sky Gilbert

QUATTRO BOOKS

Copyright © Sky Gilbert 2008

All rights reserved. No part of this book may be used or reproduced in any manner whatsoever without written permission, except in the case of brief quotations embodied in critical articles or reviews.

Cover Sculpture *Here* (1995) by Julie Campagna
Cover photo by John Calabro
Author photo by Francis Crescia
Cover Design and Typography: Julie McNeill, McNeill Design Arts

Library and Archives Canada Cataloguing in Publication

Gilbert, Sky
    Wit in love / by Sky Gilbert.

ISBN 978-0-9782806-6-6

    I. Title.

PS8563.I4743W58 2008   C813'.54   C2008-901962-8

Published by
Quattro Books
P.O. Box 53031
Royal Orchard Postal Station
10 Royal Orchard Blvd.
Thornhill, ON L3T 3C0
www.quattrobooks.ca

Printed in Canada

Wit in Love
is dedicated to Ian Jarvis

Wednesday, November 2, 1938

I am here. I assert this; or rather I should say I make the assertion. There is so much philosophical effort wasted in debate on this topic, which I will agree, seems to be important, but in fact, is not. Of course I do not mean to say that it is not important that I am here. Of course it is. If to no one else than me. But the debate over my presence is something that I am beginning to see is of relatively little importance. Who am I to prove this to? Do I need to prove my existence to the grocer or the baker or the beggar? I prove it through interaction with them, i.e. through context. It is very much the same with language. Ultimately it seems a kind of pissing contest. The philosophers are themselves very concerned about proving their own existence, while mankind goes about the day existing. But it is more than that. It is as if, somehow, it is a revelation that I am here. Or rather sitting here, in my being (how selfish that sounds!) is something that must be done. What philosophers should ponder instead of questions like "How can I prove I exist?" is "Why would I bother to question I exist?" Or even more importantly, "How does it feel not to exist?" Since it seems to me that many of us do, at times, live and feel as if we did not exist at all. Of course this is simply another discussion of Antony. For there was a time after Antony had left me, when I felt as if I did not exist. Here we have the problem of a person who situates their ontology inside another person. They have no existence outside of them. Yes, they look down and see their material body, and they talk to others, go to the store, etc. Others tell them, from their responses, "Yes you are here," but in this case that context does not provoke a response. The emptiness that one feels is enough to wipe out the sense of a personality. Or perhaps it is sadness. No, it is sadness. I think that now I have reached the point where I can experience sadness over Antony again. And it is frightening, because now that seems to me to be a good thing.

Thursday 3

How huge life's smallest irritations seem. I was waiting for the trolley bus today and there was an extensive queue. I was at the head of it. Quite proud of myself for having gotten there first, having had the due diligence, etc. So there I am feeling proud of myself and a man approaches me and asks, "Is this the bus to Topping Court?" It is, of course, as far as I know, not the bus to Topping Court. I am certain and certainly convinced that this is the bus to Swansea, for that is what the sign says (or so I thought). So I firmly answer "Swansea," since that is my understanding. I say so rather loudly, though, and this, I think at the time, is because I am being helpful and want him to hear, over the bus noise, what the destination will be. Looking back on it, I can see that I was shouting not completely out of consideration, but also partially out of annoyance – why can't people read bus signs properly? Then the woman standing behind me corrects me, obviously a bit annoyed, also. "This is the bus to Topping Court, and the bus to Swansea," she says. But this observation reports a logical impossibility. Swansea and Topping Court are not anywhere near each other and the prospect that one bus might go to both places is not a likely one. I ask the woman how this can be. She says that there is one bus to Topping Court which stops at this stop, which will soon be followed by a bus to Swansea, "How can that be?" I say. I have waited at this stop for years, ever since I moved from my father's house in Germany to my mother's house in London, it has always been the bus to Swansea, and as far back as I can remember, there has never been a time when it wasn't. "They've changed the schedule," she says. "Look at the sign." I look at the sign, and indeed, scribbled on a piece of paper beneath the large bold letters that say Swansea, someone has written Topping Court. It is nearly illegible. At this point I feel like an idiot. And I am one. So, do I apologize to the gentleman? No. Why? Because I am too embarrassed and feel too bad about myself to apologize. How many people realize this is why apologies are so often not made? If I wasn't so busy feeling bad about myself I might have had the energy to apologize to him for barking "Swansea." He seemed a nice man. Ordinary. By that I mean there was nothing memorable about him. Memorable to me, that is. This means he was not striking, or handsome, or lovely, or thoughtful, or troubled, or perhaps a combination of these things. I can't help noting my use of the word 'troubled'. Yes it does seem to me that the people who are worth knowing are troubled. By something. This does not, of course, refer to John, but that is another matter. Or should be. At any rate, the truth in this case would seem to be that the man was happy, so I did not measure him as worthy of notice. Instead I turned back to the woman – after not apologizing – and made an effort to understand the situation. In this case assuaging the feelings of someone whom I had rudely miss-corrected was much less important than figuring out exactly how a single bus could have as its terminus two such disparate destinations. The woman behind me – though she was not now behind me, for I was chatting with her and had moved beside her – began to explain the situation. It seems they had put on another bus at this stop. Hence the sign, which refers to two separate buses. Very confusing. The bus that was in front of us loaded people on to Topping Court – including the unmemorable gentleman – and I was left with my lady friend who was becoming increasingly annoyed at how long it was taking her to get to Swansea. I tried not to be annoyed too.

Friday 4

Today was a frustrating meeting with Nigel concerning Quentin's thesis. When it comes down to it, our discussion has very little to do with Quentin, in fact has nothing to do with him at all. Nigel is a fascinating old coot and someone should write about him. I find this an odd statement in itself and wonder about the extent to which people do actually model themselves after characters in novels. Not necessarily specific novels or novelists – e.g., Dickens comes to mind – but instead how often they might model themselves after the idea of being a character in a novel. What is a character in a novel? A collection of linked, easily identifiable traits, so that when one picks up the book in a bath after a day away, one can immediately say, "Oh that was Gustaf, the one who sneezes in arrogance" or "That was Ermigard, who twitches with nervousness," so that all their character traits can be easily summoned up by recognizable physical details. I have often thought that certain people nurture carefully studied behaviours because they wish to be known for possessing 'character' which means in a sense to 'be' a character, i.e. to be memorable. This is not necessarily the case, of course; they may simply be that way. People may be extreme; in fact they often are. The question is, why? It probably has to do with art and life bouncing off each other. Of course art is supposed to come from life and be an imitation of it, but I wouldn't be surprised if life imitates art now and then too, if only because it is so tempting. Apropos of Dickens I think only of my dear aged mother, who so doted on Dickens near the end of her life (I am almost certain that Dickens kept her mind off English casualties in the Boer War – many of whom, tragically, were her friends). She used to go on about "The characters…The characters! Are they not just so well observed, what detail, what realism!" Meanwhile I couldn't but help remark on the condescension in her tone. Mother loved these characters in Dickens because she could look down on them, because she obviously wasn't one of them – as she was a real person – and could not be summarized by a gesture, or catchy turn of phrase, or vocal quirk. But of course she could very well have been. Which brings me back to Nigel. The best thing to do would not be to think about him at all. But I must, because there is the student Quentin to be considered. At the moment Nigel is not considering him at all, in fact he is placing major blocks in the student's way. I had to call him and set up a meeting. Nigel was very relaxed about that. He is never openly loath to do anything, for that would place him in a powerless position. He is never angry; he is often, however, vexed or petulant. "Oh do we have to meet with precocious young Quentin? He's so pushy about his damned thesis." Well yes he is, of course he is. Wouldn't you be? I know I was, when I finally decided to hand one in. Perhaps it is a side effect of being an older single gentleman like Nigel, one who has never admitted (shall we say?) what must surely be his romantic preferences. It can't be all a bed of roses; I'm sure it isn't. But it just seems so predictably ungenerous, when one has the power, to simply, well – to wield it. Obvious and cruel. When we were having lunch, a lady vacated a seat at an adjacent table just after she was about to sit down, simply so that Nigel could have more room. I made a point of commenting upon this to Nigel. "That was kind," I said to him. I stressed the word kind. It seemed to me to be an unfamiliar word to use around Nigel. I doubt he often muses on the concept. He looked at me oddly, but I don't think it registered.

Sunday 6

Spent the whole day working at my office outside of Cambridge. This office is a particularly frustrating place. Yes I have my window and my view, and I am shaded from observance by the trees. The office is a luxurious one for unfashionable Camden Town, which I am guilty about – like so many things. I should look into the matter of guilt one day. I don't mean in a Freudian manner, surely we've already had enough of that, no. I do not wish to know why I am guilty, nothing could be more boring or useless, and in fact impossible to discover. What is however interesting is the concept of guilt. Unlike love, which has a purpose, guilt is particularly ineffable and at the same time enormously powerful. For instance, I have no doubt that certain people die from guilt, whereas others do not. There are those who could and do kill effortlessly without impunity – one hears of the bodies in an alley (there was one just the other day, in Piccadilly) of the endless, so often female, victims. Those who kill in this manner are another breed, one almost wishes to say another species. I see this in the faculty lounge when Mortimer drops a piece of paper on the floor and doesn't pick it up. I am not castigating Mortimer, though I so often do – in my own head (if there is such a place). At any rate, I have nothing against the fellow fundamentally, but he will drop a piece of paper on the floor and leave it there. This is not murder of course. But in my mind – there we are in my mind again – there is an equivalency. Of course it is not a question of moral equivalency. But there is a type of soul which always leaves a mess, whether it be a bloody mess or simply a piece of paper, for others to clean up. And if you were to tell Mortimer he would look at you charmingly in that absent way he has. "Yes, so sorry, didn't notice." And one is always suspicious, did he notice? But of course the alarming but true fact is that he did not notice, that the very thing that would drive me to distraction means nothing to Mortimer at all. I really do think it means nothing. Similarly a murder so often means nothing to a murderer – whereas I would be wracked with guilt before and after. Not that I can imagine doing such a thing. But if I could, that's the way I would be. But to get back to my office. I feel guilty about it because I am prone to guilt, but also for a valid reason. I don't need it. It is an extravagance, I am spending money unnecessarily. There is something fundamentally corrupting about ignoring money, the inequities which characterize life and differentiate people. So few have money for one office, why should I have two? And the only reason I have two is because the one at Cambridge is unsatisfactory to me because it feels public. It is in fact typical of my relationship to students that I would rather not be around them except when I am teaching. Even then it can be difficult. I know I must have my office hours, and I do. But to be there at other times, working – no, that would be impossible. And I know that I should be like Mortimer, who sits every day with his door open – he never closes his door – with the lights off and candles burning. Yes, candles. His office is a kind of Cambridge sanctuary – very appealing – and with the curtains closed the room is always dark even on the brightest day. He talks with students endlessly. I admire him for this, I do; he is being a true teacher; a friend, a mentor. I know I am a mentor to many but I don't deserve it, and do nothing to live up to it, and it is a kind of indecency that students treat me this way – someone who cares so little about them. Not like Mortimer. Oh, to be Mortimer! I was at a faculty student gathering once – I hardly ever go to those events – and I observed Mortimer with an incoming student. He was exemplary. He walked up to the lad and, smiling, purred, "Hello, I am Mortimer, and who are you?" The student was obviously thrilled and a warm discussion ensued, with Mortimer asking him where his undergraduate work was done and countless other things. Afterwards I turned to Mortimer with envy and said, "I'm amazed, I could never do that." This was the wrong thing to say. Mortimer took umbrage and raised himself to his full five foot seven inches, which is still slightly taller than me. "I find it very difficult," he said. "I am, in fact, enormously shy." Now this is something that I doubt. It seems to me a case of trying to speak my language, of appropriating what Mortimer sees as a superior attitude. I did not mean to condescend to Mortimer, and what I said was simply a visceral expression of disgust at my own inability to socialize and my horror at what actual socializing might entail. But Mortimer took it as evidence of my worldview, that socializing is a bad thing, or more specifically an inferior thing, a signal of inferiority. It was as if I was misquoting Nietzsche and characterizing myself as a Superman who could not deign to talk to people because it was beneath me. Well, that is simply not true. I do honestly loathe myself for not being able to do what he does. And I do admire him if he has triumphed over real personal hardship, i.e. shyness, in order to present a cordial face to incoming students. I was simply making the observation that chatting, being friendly, making small talk was, sadly, something which I am simply not capable of doing. At any rate, though I do not actually loathe students, and have nothing against them really, I require solitude to write anything, even this. I certainly cannot think or work when they are around. This is why I find teaching so difficult. For me, teaching should entail actual scientific discovery; in fact it should be a process in which I work through ideas in front of the students, and this I find very difficult to do, although I do somehow manage to do it quite regularly. But no, to have students around all the time would be unbearable. So I rented a room in Camden Town from a landlord who rents cheaply. I impressed him by availing myself of my title – doctor. So that is what he and everyone else there call me – doctor. They perhaps think I have a medical practice. Of course I would never use the pretentious prefix except for actual immediate material or practical gain, for which it is occasionally useful. The room is nothing, it is clean and simple. There is a small bay window where I work that looks out on the street, but sitting there at my desk I am hidden by an expansive tree. There is another window that is square, and high up, for no other reason than to let the light in. I have a desk and water and a mattress on the floor. All would be perfect except for the other man who lives on the same floor. Yes, he lives in a room down the hall and we share the bathroom. Sometimes, I cannot believe the power this little man has over me. And I do not completely understand why. Although I have my suspicions. He is the most pitiful of creatures. As I write this I wonder at my arrogance. We only pity that which we fear, for the obvious reason that we never wish to be objects of pity ourselves. So I fear Pyotor, in fact am incredibly frightened of him, which makes a perfect office so often into a nightmare. He is most certainly a character out of Kafka – a writer of whom I have never been fond, but only because I have always felt his creations did not require the fantasies that he created for them. Real human life is horrifying enough without the metamorphosis. Pyotor is an object lesson in loneliness. First, as would be required of such a lesson, he has absolutely no idea how lonely he is. This is *de rigeur* for such a person. I'm sure if you asked him if he was lonely – something one would never do – he would deny it vehemently, and speak of all his friends. Indeed he has countless friends. He sits on the step every day, for he has not got a proper job but has been hired by the landlord to be a kind of superintendent for our small building. As people walk by they become his unwitting victims. He has a 'hello' for everyone, as they say, always a cheery word. He can start a conversation about anything, but usually it is the weather. Endless musing about the cloud cover, the possibility of rain, or the mud that has been spattered on the sidewalk. He feels it is his duty to clean up such things, in fact I have often seen him sweeping the sidewalk in front of the building. I have no doubt that there are those in the neighbourhood who take a more circuitous route home to avoid him. I wish I could avoid him. He always has a word for me, something to say, whether it be, "I've left the front door unlocked, so please don't lock it behind you," which is self evident, but which nevertheless he feels compelled to remark upon, or, "Lots of traffic today, I've never seen so much traffic." And one doesn't know how to respond to such a remark, "Yes there is a lot of traffic." Or I suppose one could start up a lively contentious discussion, "No there is no traffic today," "Yes there is. I have seen several motorcars." "I have not." Etc. Of course with no one ever bothering to define exactly what a lot of traffic actually is. At any rate this is the kind of conversation he makes with me, all and sundry, anyone who will listen to him. I am not being fair. Though I find his behaviour unbearable, he may actually have some friends. I have heard him shouting in a very loud voice on the telephone in a foreign language – he has a heavy Slavic accent, either Russian or Polish – late on Sunday evenings. And I have no doubt that some of the people he talks to do consider him a friend. I have seen some of those whom he accosts on the street pause for a considerable length of time and smile while they listen to him. But it seems to me that having friends means actually making appointments with them. I am not claiming to be an expert on friends; I am very inept at finding and keeping them, which is perhaps why I am so obsessed with Pyotor and his pathetic attempts at human contact. But it seems to me that having actual friends means soliciting a time commitment from them, not continually catching them on the fly. On top of all of this he has a particularly repulsive body – he is very thin, perhaps tubercular, with greying wisps of hair all over his chest – which he displays *ad nauseum* in the hallway, even in the dead of winter. I have never known him to wear a shirt when strolling the hallway past my door. There is also a repellent smell that emanates from him. It is not something as simple as body odour or the smell of human feces, I almost wish it were. It is instead an indistinguishable and complicated smell, probably a mixture of his own human smell and cigarette smoke, for he smokes constantly – but only when he is alone in his room. I am further upset by the fact that I have the best room on the floor, which I only visit a few times a week when I require solitude – or at least to be away from students – but his room is small and tucked away at the side of the building with a tiny window. And he actually lives in it. To top it all off, his door is never closed. And he has placed a mirror just inside his room by the door, so that when one passes by his room one can see everything going on there. I have to make a great effort to turn my head away as I pass by his doorway, for fear I will see him naked in the mirror. Or worse yet just sitting, in his one chair, smoking, by his tiny window. And finally – there always seems to be more – he constantly plays very loud music, but music of the most repellent kind. I would imagine it is some kind of folk music of his native land. But it is loud, raucous, and tastelessly cheerful. Here I betray my prejudices, indeed my entire description of Pyotor betrays my prejudices. For as I'm sure you can see there, but for the grace of God go I. Pyotor is, in fact, me. He is stalking me. He is my shadow. True, it is very hard to find another office at this price. But even if I could find another office – would I? I'm not entirely sure. It is important for me to see Pyotor and to be reminded of him. It is a kind of penance.

Tuesday 8

It was a particularly odd class today. Very odd. I completely lost track of what I was saying during the first five minutes. Very unlike me. I apologized of course. I wish I could say it was due to something momentous, news of impending war, Hitler's latest troop movements, for instance. But it was for the most stupid and frivolous of reasons. I was attempting a review of my observations on language and I used the sentence – "It is most certainly over with 'A'" as an example. I cannot imagine why I would have made reference to Antony's name in this way – it was certainly not intentional – after all, I just picked 'A' because it is the first letter of the alphabet. But nevertheless I had no idea of how this would affect me; I quickly became confused and overwhelmed with sadness. It was unbearable, and I literally stopped thinking and panicked. And I had nothing to say. One suddenly has the feeling in these situations that one is somewhere else. And one doesn't just wish it, one feels transported. I am suddenly out of my body and in another space. It is not a pleasant feeling. The only thing I could think of to do was apologize, which I did profusely. I told them that I was a bad teacher, which indeed I am, for using a letter of the alphabet that calls up a name with personal associations in a linguistic example, if nothing else. But of course I couldn't tell them that. Then I went on quite normally, and I think actually was perhaps eloquent, or at least approached eloquence. A student was late. He has never been late before. I can't tolerate this and berated him; it makes no sense to me at all that students should be late for a class. They complain that they don't understand what I'm talking about, but they so often aren't even there to hear it. So I castigated him for it. He sat down and then proceeded to raise his hand more than four times during class. I didn't know what to think of his questions. Not that I didn't know how to answer them, I didn't know quite what to think of him for asking them, as they were the comical sort of philosophical questions like, "Does my hand exist?" I suppose students have been taught that this is a serious philosophical question and must ask it. I tried to make him understand the twists and turns of linguistic games that got him to a situation where he might ask such a questions. And I talked a little bit about doubt. Since the lecture concerned aesthetics I went on to discuss a recent American movie that I had seen – *Going Hollywood*. I do not usually discuss films with my students but it seemed a useful tool to illustrate the idea that responses to art are not logical, but more truly a matter of taste. Well this lecture must have given the student an idea, because immediately after class he approached me and asked if I would like to go to see a film with him. It was very odd. Of course I would never go to a movie with an undergraduate student, but since he is a graduate student and almost quite elderly – i.e., he must be nearly thirty – there was not an ethical problem. Then there were the feelings that this suggestion raised in me, for which I was not fully prepared. I think it was his manner of dress. There was something slightly wrong there. I know there is something wrong with the way I dress; I know this, for instance, because I once overheard two students discussing my appearance. I had come into the doorway of the classroom behind them and they could not see me, and one of the students used the word 'shabby' to describe me. This was not disturbing; merely interesting. And then the other one said, "He looks a bit like a tramp, doesn't he; sometimes I get the feeling we're being taught by a tramp." At this point I thought the discussion had gone too far and might prove embarrassing for all of us. I coughed and looked down as if I was wiping my wet feet in the doorway and proceeded into the room. There was much giggling and shushing, but the students did not know that I had overheard them. Alone in my rooms later, I examined myself in the mirror and noted that indeed, there was something shabby about me. On closer inspection I discovered that not only was my jacket old and frayed at the edges but one of the pockets was ripped. Now this was something that I knew – i.e., had some sort of cognizance of. But I did not, in another way, actually know it at all. Re: the process of knowing – are there some things that we know but do not know, because we take them for granted? This falls into the same category as having arms. I know I have arms but I do not think of it, so if someone were to ask me if I had arms I would say yes, but there would be a necessary pause, to ponder. Which of course is where doubt comes in – because suddenly one is thinking about something one never thinks about. What I'm getting at here is those things that we take for granted we may sometimes believe don't really exist. So on the one hand I was aware that the pocket of my coat was ripped, but on the other hand I never thought about it. So to actually think about it, that became the surprise. But the observation that I was shabby was not hurtful or upsetting to me. To be called shabby is simply the result of a particular, subjective, almost meaningless judgement – i.e., what is shabby, to you, is casual, or even picturesque, to someone else. But the 'tramp' characterization affected me profoundly. I do not like to think of myself as a tramp. Why? What is a tramp? Two things specifically: a poor person and one with no direction in life. The first part I have no problem with. I am poor and I have chosen that and no state could bring with it more dignity. I have enormous respect for the poor; in fact they deserve our admiration so much more than those who have never had to struggle for anything. But to lack direction, to be aimless, purposeless, all of this brings me the highest anxiety. I would rather not be this kind of tramp. But of course in a way I am. How long has it been since I have published a book – nearly twenty years! So in this way this silly student gossip affected me and I still think of it. And maybe they were right, maybe their teacher is a kind of tramp. But it also occurred to me that there is another way that I am a tramp, and that is simply by being a thinker – and by this I merely mean someone who spends a lot of his time thinking, nothing else. I am not making a value judgement – because I am a thinker, I simply have no time to bother with pockets. My ripped pocket was merely a cosmetic problem; after all, it was still deep enough to hold loose change and paper clips. So when the student asked me to see a film with him, I happened to notice his manner of dress. His pants were too short, revealing an unattractive pair of white socks. And also – and this is the painful thing – he too had a ripped pocket. After observing this, the stab of feeling was so great, it was as if someone had punched me in the stomach. The feeling was not simply a feeling, it was the result of a very quick thought process. For I had made this connection: "Oh he has a ripped pocket and I have a ripped pocket. Therefore we are similar." And the assumption continued to flower: "We are similar in the way that we are both thinkers, the kind of thinkers who have no time to think about trivial things." I am not at all certain from the questions that this young man asked in class that he thinks deeply about anything. But from the glimpse of his torn pocket I had stolen a sad and wretched hope.

Wednesday 9

I am very angry with my brother. In a letter he raves about Strauss's *Elektra*. It is not his fault that music means so much to him; he would be dead by now if it weren't for music. For this reason I don't send him a rant against the man who now appears to be his favourite composer. He tells me that a newly conducted version of the opera is a "revelation." He wishes to send me the record. I can think of nothing more horrifying. Anything after Brahms upsets me; makes me angry. I have no doubt that the world is out of joint; I see evidence of it everywhere. I have no need to find this reflected in music, especially Strauss with all that screeching. This really is the one thing that makes me very angry. I don't want to be angry, especially with my brother, because it seems he is always barely hanging on. I know it all makes sense – his life is desperate, he plays the piano beautifully and desperately, there is beauty also in that desperation. So now I must go through the moral dilemma of whether or not to write him a letter and agree. I always find this difficult. The number of compromises that one must make for any simple human interaction. It shouldn't matter to me, I never see my brother, I could lie and tell him that I am buying the damned record, I could even lie and tell him that I liked it. I think it also has to do with the fact that he insists on ignoring my feelings, he knows that I don't have his taste in music and then insists that I get excited over something that he knows I could never get excited about. It's an incredible, gargantuan selfishness. Or perhaps I am the selfish one, when I think how little the lie would matter that might make him happy. But why apologize for melody? Music critics fall over themselves with embarrassment when they encounter it: "Rachmaninoff here finds himself chained to those romantic melodies." Melodies are the embodiment of love, and to live in a world without melody is to live in a world without love. This is not a world that I would choose to live in. Thinking the other day about Antony and the phrase I could have used about him in class, the insane phrase I might have used: "He was everything to me." One knows that this is not true. It is not even healthy, that someone should be everything to anyone. Don't we all need a variety of influences and associations in our lives? I know that I do. Would I have met John for instance, if Antony had lived? And I must keep reminding myself that I would have been much less fond of Antony if he had not died. How difficult it is for me to write that. After I write it I think it is some kind of betrayal and cannot be true. The only truth is that I have such strong emotions about him that I don't know what I really think, or if I can really think at all about him. But when I ponder what I actually mean by saying "He means everything to me" I realize that what I am feeling is more about myself than about him. For I am describing the feeling of only being truly alive when I'm with him. I'm thinking of that day we played chess. That very first day. It has to do with the fact that I respected so much his opinions about everything. And now looking back on it I think – was he really as deep as all that? Was it just perhaps his voice? He had a very deep voice. Or perhaps it was a kind of jaded attitude, very world-weary for one so young. And I was young too, and so much more naive. There is a bench near Great Ormond Street Hospital for Children where he said good-bye to me.

Even after all this time I still go there. It is insanity on my part, sheer insanity. I circle around it on my bicycle. It is a particular bench. I cannot believe that the bench is not gone. That was now over ten years ago. I will approach the bench but I will not be able to sit. For after all, he did not simply say good-bye, even though it seemed like good-bye. He said something much more cruel. It still has a perversely magical quality, that bench. I don't know why I go back there. It is the way we return to a sad melody. Noel Coward, the comedian, says in one of his plays, "It is extraordinary how potent cheap music is." By cheap music, he means music with melody. It is like apologizing over and over again for being in love. Here again I am like Pyotor who lives beside my office. He plays those insipid polka tunes endlessly – I don't know if they are polka tunes but they all sound like polkas to me – so loudly and with his door wide open. One day I asked him, very politely I thought under the circumstances, "Might it be possible for you to turn down the music?" "Why, no," he said. "No. I must have my music. I couldn't live without my music!" And so it is for all of us, I think.

Thursday 10

Another meeting with Nigel, this time with Quentin present, concerning Quentin's thesis. Quentin squirmed in his chair somewhat, which is typical under the circumstances. I can't tell whether he is up to it, brilliant though he may be. He had to be prompted about so many things; they were the usual things. He wished to write a book such as Bertrand Russell might write – he even cited Russell. But we pointed out that this was perhaps not possible and certainly not desirable at this stage. I wisely didn't go on about what Russell has become, it didn't seem prudent or politic. Or more accurately, I didn't want to be cruel. It is simply sad when people don't live up to their potential. Potential is a fictitious thing; what we really mean when we speak of potential is that people don't live up to the dreams we had for them. I have no dreams for Quentin – I just hope he isn't wasting our time. I was very irritated with Nigel again because he insisted on insulting me. Why? What is there that he has to prove? It's as if he is laying out the bait, and there's no reason for me to take it, except in the name of reason itself. Suddenly out of nowhere he said, in an almost offhand way, his voice lowered, wiping the spittle out of his mouth (why is he always spitting?), "Since we know that mathematical logic describes the world...." I couldn't believe my ears. And we had been getting along so well. I had been deferring to Nigel, which means speaking first, and then remaining silent. I had asked him if he wanted to speak first; he didn't want to, which makes perfect sense. How much easier in such situations, to be the one who sits and is critical of the one who speaks first! This he did. After criticizing my ideas about Quentin, he proceeded to humiliate him, saying things like "And do you actually want to pass your thesis? Do you actually have the fantasy of becoming a doctor?" Of course the student holds that fantasy, he is sitting in my office. And then he drones on and on. I begin to examine the wallpaper in my office walls, which is decorated with flowers of such intricate detail that one could go quite mad looking at them. But I am fine with it; Nigel wishes to be in charge of the interrogation, there is nothing wrong in that, I can certainly let him. Then in the middle of his drone, he unleashes an astounding remark about logic. Of course it is only astounding to me, not so much to anyone else, but Nigel knows perfectly well that I abandoned logic as a description of reality years ago, and have begun to move into a sceptical analysis of language. So then it becomes a test of wills. Am I to let this remark pass? I very well could, in the sense that it doesn't matter. But then it does. It's not fair to Quentin because I certainly don't want him thinking that I have boundless faith in the ability possessed by logic to describe the world. So, necessarily, when I begin to speak again I say, "I must take issue with you Nigel." And I proceed to do so. But he won't give up. When it is his turn to speak he swings back to the topic, defending logic, and suggesting this time that logic's relationship to the world is sometimes difficult to prove. At this point the session is threatening to dwindle into an argument between the two us when instead it should be a discussion about Quentin. I look over at him and I think, to his credit, that he is thankful to me for not placing logic on a pedestal. But he may simply be afraid of Nigel, and just relieved that I am there. If only Quentin wasn't young and attractive, perhaps Nigel wouldn't be so mean to him. When it is all over I lock up my office and start on the way home. On my way out the door I pass Tristan's office. Tristan is a young poet who occupies the office downstairs. He is sitting in his rooms with the curtains only partially closed. Sunlight is streaming through the windows, because it is just before sunset. He is making paper airplanes and launching them about the room from behind his desk. He is a very tiny man, meticulous in his dress and demeanour. I smile at him, but something about the scene irks me deeply. It might just be bad feelings lingering from the meeting with Nigel and Quentin but I don't think so. What irks me about Tristan is the most trivial thing. But it says so much. He is in the habit of leaving his office door open when he is not there. This is in spite of the fact that we have been told endlessly by the Cambridge dons that it is unwise – furthermore that it is foolish in the extreme – not to lock our office doors at all times. Tristan leaves his door wide open when he goes off to class. I have noticed his door sitting open for hours at a time. And one never knows where he is. He is mostly out of his office, even when he is not teaching class, and so his office has a kind of ghostly presence. I often see his jacket draped over the chair, and his umbrella leaning against the desk, as if he had abandoned them suddenly, as if there had been an earthquake or a hurricane and he had been swallowed by the ground or swept away by a gust of wind. His office always appears as if he had just been there. It must be very frustrating for the students. But it is more than that. It's not just that he is inaccessible to his students and indeed everyone. Nor is it that he is remarkably foolhardy to leave his office for hours at time. No, it is that his action indicates a kind of trust in the world, a faith in the very goodness at the core of everything, which I must honestly say that I envy. His trust is lambent, there is something brilliant about it; it glows. What is all the more astounding is that Tristan has no reason to feel this way. For as a tiny meticulous man, he had been, actually – quite recently in fact – the victim of a campus stalking. Nothing came of it, but apparently a student followed him home late one evening, after dusk, and cornered him, threatening to beat him to a pulp before Tristan somehow escaped. Tristan had given a description of the culprit to the authorities, but no trace of a student of that description could be found. What I'm getting at is this: Tristan's trust in the world is completely unjustified, at least in what appears to be his experience of it. Yet everything about him invites disaster, from his height to his meticulousness, to leaving his office open, to his sweet smile, and to his excessive politeness. And there he sits in his office launching paper airplanes at dusk. The world that I experienced at his age was so much easier, in the sense of being born into wealth. Tristan leaving his office open reminds me very much of the time when I decided to work in an army hospital. Of course the horror of what I encountered there is nothing compared to leaving one's office open. But what I'm trying to say is that Tristan appears to trust the world. It is a *Chaplinesque* quality that I thought only existed in American films. I don't trust the world and I expect it to kill me at any moment, but I only occasionally, and very carefully, put myself in harm's way. Yet he sails about, blissfully unafraid.

Friday 11

Arthur (the graduate student with a torn pocket) came by to arrange a movie for us to see. I am struck by how strangely thin he is, and by his very adult-looking beard – not fully grown, but covering the lower part of his face. This makes his eyes stand out with an alarming quality; very alive and sparkling. It is obvious to me that Arthur idolises me to some degree. This is not odd, it is something that many students do. He suggested that we go and see a film called *Grand Hotel*. It does not sound like the kind of film that would interest me; my favourite films are Busby Berkeley musicals. The more bizarre the better. If I am going to enter another world I want that world to have its own rules so I can't possibly use my own standards to judge it. When watching it, I want there to be no escape. On the contrary, Grand Hotel sounds like the most common brand of melodrama. But Arthur seems set on it, so I agree. We will see it next Tuesday, since I have no classes on Wednesday. On Arthur's way out of my office a very sad thing happened. Quentin was waiting outside my door to discuss his thesis with me for the thousandth time. He seemed very unhappy at seeing me with Arthur. Or precisely, envious. I knew that he was aware of Arthur's obvious adoration for me. I could tell instantly – how does one know these things? – that this was the kind of adoration he wanted for himself, and that it was the sole reason why he was pursuing his studies. It became painfully apparent to me in that moment that Quentin has no interest in truth or knowledge or inquiry, but very much wishes that he could be me – well, he is young and beautiful; he might as well be ambitious too. This does not mean that I will fail him, it means that I am disappointed by his reasons for pursuing an academic career.

Saturday 12

I recently reread my journal entry of Wednesday the 9th, which is perhaps something I should not do. The purpose of a journal is to have the opportunity to think out loud, which one can't do when one is censoring oneself – the result of going back and reading it again. But there was something about my entry on that day that bothered me. I knew that I had returned to Antony, and gone somewhat mad. But when I reread it, I was astounded by the unabashed sentimentality of it all. My objection to sentimentality is not moral, it is aesthetic. But also perhaps it is a matter of truth – whatever truth means. The idea of truth, the intention of truth. Sentimentality is not about truth. If one looks at the history of art, one is struck by the contrast in output between those periods which are ruled by sentimentality and those which are not. During the 18th century, for instance, unreason ruled, in the guise of 'the sentiments'. Adam Smith's *Theory of Moral Sentiments* is a particularly annoying document, for he posits that we are naturally predisposed to sympathy for those who do good things, and to reward them, and to respond angrily when those who do bad things receive the same approbation. This is only true if one is a good person. It's nice to assume that we are all good people, and the philosopher's confident "we," i.e., "We all respond positively when," must be immediately suspect, for what "we" is this specifically? The philosopher always assumes he is speaking to a sympathetic audience of good people and not to an unsympathetic audience of madmen. In fact I much prefer Oscar Wilde's statement – which I can only paraphrase – something to the effect of, "The good ended well and the bad ended badly, that is what fiction is." How, basically, can one be sentimental when one is thinking persistently, about anything? This is the early Wilde, the Wilde of *The Importance of Being Earnest*. One must never read *De Profundis*, because it is the very opposite sort of document, a repudiation of his own wit, of reason even, and a defence of all the most sentimental virtues, love, duty, etc. I don't mean of course to identify wit with reason or even to suggest that reason is necessarily a good thing. I'm not making a moral distinction. I do not have boundless faith in science. At any rate, I prefer Wilde, Shakespeare, Goethe or the Greeks, who (though not all usually classified as wits, nevertheless) had a hard-edged, thoughtful, uncompromising concept of reality. This is why I like Busby Berkeley musicals and the very first talkies. They have an edge to them that is unbesmirched by sentimentality, a craziness that resembles reality at its most abrasive – all very unlike the kind of movies they are making now, and what I fear this film *Grand Hotel* will be. And when I look back at my Wednesday 9th entry – which I will never do again – it seems to me that I was wallowing in a kind of sentimentality that is not only silly but dangerous. I think it is time for a visit to my sister. There is so much I despise about her. But that is what I need. Not Hermoine, of course, I don't need any of that right now – in its own way that would be more of the same. What I need is a good strong dose of Griselda. She is so aptly named – the one who waits – and though so much of what she represents I despise, seeing her would put the perfect edge to my life. Yes, there is a sense in which she is the worst kind of sentimental woman, her house, for instance, is a Biedermeier nightmare, and her taste – her execrable taste! But she confronts reality every day in the sense of having children and feeding them, and watching them grow and wail. And then there is her religion, which I can't hate because after all it makes sense to her. Visiting Griselda is a kind of hair shirt. I remember how much Antony hated her, how he made fun of her, how she spurred a wit in him, a wit of the most bitter kind. For that very reason I must go and visit her, because when I visit her I cannot think of him.

Sunday 13

I am here. I can confidently say that. Griselda lives only two hours from London and she is always glad to see me. As I a lie in the bedroom of this extravagant country mansion and the sunlight streams in, I reflect on the knowledge that her husband has always, always lived in this house. He spent his childhood here and now his children are growing up here too. He has never known anything else. His sensibility, his perceptions of the world, have been significantly bounded. He is a country doctor, and I wanted to dislike him on sight. I remember when I met him ten years ago – it was in fact with Antony before we went on one of our trips to Norway. I knew only what Griselda had told me about him in letters – about what a solid man he was, and how responsible and respectable he was, and all those things which mean nothing, at least to me. I was fully prepared to hate him. And then when I got to this place – for this is where he is, there is nowhere else – I found a vast library. He reads. Well, of course, he is intelligent. But there are many intelligent people who don't. And what does he read? Well interestingly enough, in light of what thoughts led me here, nothing later than the early nineteenth century. Being English, he adores Adam Smith and Jane Austen. It is very much like reading children's books. But I admire that, a brain that says: "This is as far as I would like to go, I don't wish to be challenged in any further way." It's like my taste in music – I am frightened if I wander too far away from Brahms, I am suddenly venturing out on a cliff where I might fall, or down a trail where I might wander too far and never find my way home. He is a kind man, and that is all my sister wishes for. Watching their piousness is a fascinating sort of trial for me. It is not ostentatious – but yet it is. For their prayers before meals require a certain complicity from guests and are a kind of performance. We all hold hands, and close our eyes. There is a part of me that wants to not close my eyes, to not hold hands with the person beside me, to not recite these words that I find objectionable merely because they are meaningless. I am not going to remind them that there isn't a God because I think that is a nonsensical sort of statement. For how can it be proved? It is the inappropriateness of using logical analysis and argument for metaphysical questions that has given metaphysicians a bad name. So I see nothing wrong with them praying, just as I see nothing wrong with them sleeping or eating; these are all things this family obviously needs to do. As religious as they are, their thought processes are more than practical – they are pragmatic. They take what they need from religion, and they need parts of *The Bible*, not those passages that smell of moral uncertainty – certain of Christ's statements about prostitutes for instance – but notions that suit their sensibility and seem useful for bringing up children. Over the hallway that leads to a room that they call the parlour is an archway, on which there is written, "Welcome to our Christian home." I am trying desperately not to hate this sign. Why bother? Because, despite the braggadocio of these banners, despite the obvious self-righteousness, they really do seem like nice people. I don't dislike them. They don't dislike me. They try and include me in their discussions, because their family is all-important to them. The two little girls are not at the age – approaching ten years old – where they are beginning to have fantasies of marriage and wish to imagine getting dressed up in a pretty way. The boy is younger and still just a boy. Sometimes I think it is because of the bad record of the boys in our family – that two of my brothers are suicides – that they are able to put up with me without complaint. After all, what is it I *do* exactly? I *think* for a living. This *must* be suspect. And what is my society? I don't seem to have any. Why do I live? In the context of their very orderly lives, this would seem a reasonable question to ask. They have lived to procreate, to heal, to love, to further the species, and to amass objects which will make their surroundings beautiful and comfortable. I wish I could say that they are complacent, evil people but I do not think so. Only perhaps a little boring. I could not imagine remaining here for more than a day that is without something specific to do. And Griselda is intent, as she always is, whenever I come, that I should come more often and stay longer. This makes no sense to me, we have so little in common, and yet seem to get along so well now, seeing each other hardly ever. And then she makes the suggestion, or should I say, ventures out to sea, first testing the waters. "We are dissatisfied," she says, "with our house." I find this a shocking revelation; this was the house where her husband was born, after all. "He is dissatisfied too. It's not large enough for the children." Well, it's true that although the house is large in the sense that the ceilings are high and the rooms are spacious, they are filled to the brim, and there are not enough rooms – only three bedrooms and no guest room. For instance, I am now sleeping in the little boy's room and he is uncomfortably ensconced with his sisters. "No" – she says, shaking her head, "the children are getting too old for this and they, understandably, need more space." My sister chats on and on about this. I am shocked that she would consider such a change to her life, and that her husband would consider moving from his birthplace. But then I realize that anything is possible for them, but only because they have children, and children bring change, and they will do anything for them. Then I find myself suggesting something which I realize, as soon as I have said it, is quite an insane thing. I immediately wish to retract my words because I'm not entirely certain why I suggested it. I'm in the unique position of not understanding my own motives. Anyway, I suggest that I might perhaps design a new home for them. Well I know why the idea came to me – in the most superficial sense, that is – I would be very good at it. It would be a good pastime for me. It would get my mind off Antony. These are all obvious, sensible reasons. Can there be another reason? I don't want to think about it, or more accurately don't know how to think about it. Well, why should I be suspicious of myself? Perhaps because I know of the enthusiasm with which they will seize the idea. Their admiration for me is endless. I have published a book, I have a position at the university. These things are beyond their imagining and make me a being from a fairy story, a brother with special powers. My sister is convulsed with joy, she claps her hands together, her ringlets bounce – I notice how much she resembles a Jane Austen heroine, and how anachronistic this is. Perhaps she styles her hair this way to satisfy her husband. At any rate, she is overjoyed and can't wait to tell him, and when he comes home from a particularly vexing appointment she does. And of course he is bursting with enthusiasm too. Well why shouldn't he be? And so am I, am I not? But I am faintly uncomfortable with myself for suggesting this. Yes I have the experience, the background, certainly, in engineering and design. Certainly the project would revitalize me; indeed I could see becoming obsessed with it in no time. But I fear that by designing the house for them I will become some kind of God. This is not a good position for anyone to be in. Even God. I promise to think about it, but I know that now that I have made the suggestion and caused all this excitement, it will be a difficult matter to do what will be seen as changing my mind, and say no. We'll see what happens.

Tuesday 15

I must set it all down. The discussion was certainly enlightening. I still don't know exactly what to think of him. I have just returned from the movie. I had no idea, first of all, that it was made six years ago, and is already a kind of classic in the United States. That shows how out of touch I am. I wish Arthur hadn't told me all this. I don't like being told anything about a film I am going to see or a book I am going to read. I want to make up my own mind about it – although making up my own mind is a conflicted phrase because it brings with it the idea of a private thinking, something which I ultimately don't think possible. Isn't it interesting the way we protect our very own little worlds which we imagine are so different from everyone else's? These worlds are different, but in a way they are not. There are limits to the way I can think differently about anything because there are limits to the language. Ultimately my language is the same as yours, and there are only certain words that we can use to speak of things, and therefore, think of them. On the other hand, it is completely possible that each person has a different experience of the world. Part of the problem is that we might never know if our experience is different, because we all have the same way of talking about it. Arthur and I speak the same language, English, which is partially a Romance and partially a Teutonic language; it has nouns and verbs and a certain style of grammar. But I'm not positive that our experience of the film was the same. Arthur liked the film, but I didn't. The film is, on the whole, a very trashy melodrama. It cannot be defended in terms of its characterizations, the likelihood of its happenings, etc. The conceit of the film is that it is about life in a hotel, real life, in a very grand hotel, and it offers poor and working class moviegoers the opportunity to spy on the fantastical lives of the very rich. In this film the lives of the rich are filled with sadness and depravity. This of course satisfies the need for schadenfreude on the part of those whose lives have been less fortunate. Although the plot concerns a collection of guests, it actually centres on Kringelein – a lowly accountant – and Preisling, a wealthy banker who is his employer. It disappointed me to see that Arthur seemed completely captivated by the film. He was sitting on the edge of his seat, and I actually saw him wipe away a tear after Grusinskaya the ballerina – played by Greta Garbo – learns of her lover's death and sinks into depression. When the lights came up Arthur was practically jumping up and down with excitement over Garbo's performance. I remained unconvinced. I have seen Greta Garbo in films before, but I don't think I have ever heard her talk. Though she has a fine, low, throaty voice, her performance was in some instances ridiculously over the top. At other moments her bizarre grimaces and maniacal gesticulations did seem uncannily appropriate, but as her character was insane, and she is a somewhat mad actress, this could easily have been by accident. What irritated me more about Arthur's response was that he not only enjoyed the trashy melodrama but made an attempt to assert that it was a serious philosophical movie. It certainly pretends to be. The narrator speaks constantly of death, but in not too subtly veiled ways. But I found anything that this character had to say hard to stomach, not because he was so clearly set up as the mouthpiece of the author, but because his scar was so unconvincing. It is not Arthur's fault that he didn't notice this, he has never been on the battlefield. But the narrator of this film sported a strawberry splash of colour on one side of a perfectly formed face, something more resembling a birthmark than an injury due to a grenade accident, which is what it was supposed to be. Also the leading man, John Barrymore, who played the ne'er-do-well Baron, wore far too much makeup. He actually sported eyeshadow! Only one character struck an emotional chord with me – Kringelein, because he reminded me of a teacher at the university – Reginald Bourne. Kringelein was the spitting image of Reginald, in fact they might have been brothers. Reginald, too, has an unattractive greying moustache. He is the type of professor that the students love – and the kind of professor I could never be – a sweet old fussbudget and kind beyond belief – but I dared not tell Arthur because it wouldn't have been right for me to offer such a condescending characterization of one of my colleagues. Another aspect of Kringelein's character struck me. Arthur was very impressed with his life philosophy, which was the dominant message of the film: "a man who doesn't know death doesn't know life." This comforting homily made me think of my sister Hermoine. She has been ill for a year now and teetering perilously close to death. It does not faze her, however, and she seems almost to relish the notion of its approach. I should have mentioned her to Arthur but instead I made a pathetic attempt to analyze the film on a more profound level – pathetic because I don't think Arthur had a clue of what I was talking about. The character of Grusinskaya falls in love with a jewel thief who has invaded her room. The night before she meets him she is contemplating suicide. After she meets him she is suddenly, inexplicably, hauling gigantic bouquets of flowers about and hurling herself towards hotel doors in fur coats. Since it is impossible to fall in love at first sight – this is a fantasy created by the movies – the extremity of her self-delusion is impressive. After all, Grusinskaya is the same person the day before she falls in love as the day after. Nothing has actually changed. But though Grusinskaya is not in love, her perception of the world has changed. This made me think about what little connection our perceptions actually have to reality. I wanted to express all this to Arthur but it wasn't fully articulated in my mind. I can't say that I am impressed with Arthur. In fact I am quite disappointed. I had dreamed too much over that damned torn pocket. I don't know whether or not I can assume from his shallow reaction to the film that he is not a thinker. Perhaps I should give him another chance. But I hold little hope for some sort of future for us as friends. If he asks me to another movie I will probably refuse him. This saddens me, so I refuse to think about it.

Wednesday 16

An afternoon of relief. When my classes ended I decided on impulse to take the train to Kew Gardens. I couldn't think of a practical reason. I simply needed to go. On reflection such impulses often make me a lot happier than the more considered ones. Anyway, there I was, and of course there is always the possibility that I will meet John on one of these trips. It is never planned. I don't check the days that he works and never have, although I will admit that it's always at the back of my mind that he might be there. Well, the train had barely pulled out of the station before John came by with the usual packets of nuts. I bought some from him and I could see that he had that lively sparkle in his eye that brings me so much relief. I cannot explain my attraction to John and don't want to. We always do the strangest things. It makes me uncomfortable when I reflect on them. Still, I want to set it down so I remember. It's important to remember those moments when one is simply existing, as opposed to thinking about existing. A few moments later John had sold all his nuts, which is his job. Job done, John's simplistic – but not simple – mind moved to the next logical conclusion. Time to have fun. He leaned over to me and whispered in a jaunty way, "Come to the last car, mate!" – pointing in the direction of the back of the train. Of course I followed him. My heart was beating wildly. This was madness! On our way to the back of that car he stopped and nodded his head towards the right and I noticed a very fat man – he was grossly overweight

– eating two bags of peanuts, one in each hand. When I looked up, John was looking at me with a devilish grin. He bolted out the door at the back of the train and I followed him through various cars. He moved very quickly, but now and then when he passed a particularly notable person he would stop briefly and nod towards them without them seeing. At one point it was a woman with large breasts that – though they were well concealed by a blouse – were nevertheless freakish. Another time it was an old man who was coughing and wheezing and drooling. John stopped and made a scowley face. He is cruel sometimes, especially about physical infirmity, but how can one hate him for it? There is simply nothing to hate in John. Finally we got to an empty car. I was surprised. I didn't think there were empty cars on trains. He immediately ripped off his coat and rolled up his shirtsleeves. I noticed that he was sweating and the sweat was clogged in the hairs on his forearms. I removed my jacket too. It occurred to me that without it, I was, for a moment at least, no longer shabby. "So what didya think?" he asked. "Of what," I said. "Of the fattie?" he asked. "He was pretty fat," I said. "Yup. Crapper tried to pinch me nuts." "He tried what?" I said, incredulous. This was one of John's jokes. He threw his had back and laughed. There is nothing quite like the sound of John's laughter – unfettered and raw. "No, the crapper tried to get away without paying for one of his bags. As if he needed two. How does the bugger take a shit?" The most practical questions always beguile John. I told him I didn't know. "I mean if he sat on the toilet his ass'd swallow it, or he'd break it." Of course this was very true. "And the lady with the bazooka guns?" I told him I didn't know what a bazooka gun was. "New kind of gun we're going to get if we have to go to war with the Germans." John is obsessed about going to war with the Germans. Of course this is possible, quite possible, but would put me in a rather awkward position, being a German in England. Does he know all this? Does he sense it? Does it matter? "And the old thing" he said referring to the drooling old man. "Why doesn't he just die, eh? Why doesn't he just die!" "I often ask myself that," I said. "What?" asked John, cocking his head as if he hadn't heard me. Only I thought he had. "Nothing," I said. "Okay," he said, hunkering down in a wrestling position opposite me on the aisle. "Are you going to let me through?" I could tell not only from his words but from the guttural catch in his voice that he wanted a fight. I hunkered down too, and rolled up my sleeves. Then and there, in the car, we wrestled. It's only a half an hour to Kew Gardens and I knew we didn't have much time left. What if someone came in on us? Was it illegal to wrestle on a train? But it didn't take him long; he always wins. In a minute or two he had me on the floor between the seats and he was panting, his full body weight – which is a considerable wall of muscle – on top of me. "Say uncle!" he shouted, squirming around. Of course I wouldn't for a while; the sensation of his firmness so close to me was too exciting. Then a whistle blew and he quickly kissed me on the lips. He had never done that before! He hopped up and yanked on his coat. "Gotta go mate," he said. And he was off. I sat on the floor in my shirtsleeves, dazed and indescribably aroused. Believe it or not I could think of nothing. It was such a pleasure. It's a wonder that a stream of people didn't come in and find me. After I walked back to my seat I did think of Einstein's theory of relativity, oddly enough. I remember one of my students once starting an answer to a question with: "Einstein's theory of relativity states that time slows down on trains." Well indeed there had just been a moment for me – after we *wrassled* – when time had stopped. Where everything had stopped. And I didn't properly know where I was.

Thursday 17

A luncheon today with Nigel – ostensibly to talk over Quentin, but really just to cure Nigel's loneliness. I have lunch with him because it's much less trouble than saying no. He started off an endless monologue about his dog Napoleon. Napoleon is an ageing Pomeranian who has had countless operations but still coughs and wheezes and drools as much as that old man John and I saw on the train. His problems are part and parcel of his breed and inevitable; Nigel loves Napoleon deeply and of course will not stand for this. He dotes on that animal, in I'm sure what Freud would call a neurotic fashion – which just proves how inept Freud can be. Freud would have Nigel on a couch in a minute, and there would, I'm sure, be impenetrable complexes and a deluge of forbidden dreams. I don't want to speculate on Nigel's sexual frustration and it is not my place to do so. Nor is it Freud's. He is happy with his dog and will even enjoy the drama of Napoleon's inevitable, messy death in his own way. But what was most disconcerting was his insistence on mentioning Arthur, and carefully examining my response. I am certain I was not imagining this. He had gone to Brighton for a couple of days to visit his ailing mother, and couldn't of course bring the dog, so he asked Arthur to stay at his flat and take care of it. He went on and on about Arthur – about how adorable he is. And then he examined my face, quite brazenly, for any hint of a reaction. I said something like "Yes, Arthur seems sweet, yes." I wonder if Nigel knows that Arthur and I have been to the movies together. I didn't tell him. Well, all the more reason not to go out with Arthur again. But this was not enough for Nigel. He said the most outrageous thing. It disgusted me. I don't understand how old men of his ilk can talk like this; I never have. It must be part of some mental disease which I'm sure Freud would be eager to diagnose. Arthur had to stay overnight at Nigel's flat when he was taking care of Napoleon, and Nigel surprised Arthur in the morning with his early return. "He was wearing his pyjamas and I think there was something going on in his pants." Then his eagle eye devoured me again for a prurient response. I had none; I do not think of Arthur in that way, and if I did it would be none of Nigel's business. I quickly changed the subject to Quentin, and Nigel informed me that Quentin has tuberculosis. I think this is significantly irrelevant but makes sense; as an undergraduate student he was always making sick excuses, and not attending class. It is sad of course. But he has a very slow moving, reversible variety of the disease, that is easily treatable, so his life is not in any immediate danger. Nigel mentioned Quentin's illness in that way people have; he wished for me to be more solicitous of the boy. And this from the fussy old man who abuses Quentin so mercilessly in our meetings! In his presence Nigel tortures Quentin but when we are alone he seeks my sweet sympathy for a tragic turn of events in young Quentin's life. I told him that I was sad to hear that Quentin was ill. This was true as far as it went. But I can't see that tuberculosis is going to make me grant him a higher mark. Quentin was catty about a colleague, which is his favourite thing to do. Then, perhaps because he wasn't able to get much of a reaction from me as of yet, he said, "I would love to have a discussion with you someday about cultural relativism." This came out of nowhere.

I hoped that he wasn't going to attempt to disagree with me; that would be so tedious. I asked him if he questioned cultural relativism. He said no, but that he was interested in its relationship to cognitive relativism. Cognitive relativism is a touchy issue and one which I am very interested in exploring. I didn't know what to say, so I fell back on my usual approach in these situations, which is to agree vaguely but set no time. "Yes we shall have to talk about that." I said. I sincerely hope we never will.

Friday 18

I left my hat on the train. A tiny incident; it should mean nothing. Some events only seem to have meaning because we attribute feelings to them that affect our perceptions. It was a battered hat. I hardly ever wore it. I had been invited to deliver a lecture in Leamington; it was necessary for me to arrive wearing headgear. I lost my hat the way one always loses things. The very moment that I stepped off the train and the doors closed I realized that I had left it on the seat. Nothing to be done, no porter anywhere – no hope. This caused me to reflect on death. Losing a hat is like death, for death can be so sudden. One day the person is beside you and then you turn around and they are gone. Then, because I was thinking of death, there was a flood of feeling over Antony. Out of nowhere on this gloomy day I experienced such a sudden rush of emotion that I nearly swooned. The only way I could quell the onslaught was to remind myself that my memory of him was not real. It could not be; memories by definition are not. We were young. What is youth but a collection of perfect moments that become more perfect as the years go by? I look at pictures of Antony now – standing by a rock near a mountain, for instance – and he does not seem so terribly beautiful. Indeed in one picture I appear much more handsome than he. I know that he was callow, that he treated me in a callow way, was cold, insensitive, and deliberately hurtful at times. I relished this, for I could play the heroine of a romantic opera. I remember how, after we quarrelled,

I would find myself lurking in the darkest alleys where the silliest boys would linger – all in revenge for some trivial wrong he had done me. These days, all is transmogrified when, clearing a pile of papers from my desk, I suddenly come upon a card he sent me, or when I for no reason suddenly remember a teasing prank he pulled – one that proved that he *must* have loved me. I remember with aching fondness how we used to argue over Brahms. At the time it was simply enough to find someone who cared enough about Brahms to get into an argument over him. But I must stop thinking about Antony. Some things are impossible. There are moments in life that we think have occurred but they are only make-believe.

Saturday 19

I had to visit Hermoine because the film about the ballerina had made me think about my older sister. Also it was time. Hermoine would never invite me to visit; this would be beyond her, she is always too ill. She has been ill for years. With what, we do not know. Or rather, we knew once, but we have long since forgotten. And her list of ailments has become so extensive that it's best not to inquire about them anymore. She mentions, in passing, "Oh, I was on the toilet all day yesterday," or "I find that lately I can barely walk." But she will not see a doctor. So there is suffering, endless suffering which she complains of, but hers is not to wonder why, hers is simply to suffer. If you inquire too much after her health she cries, "Why are you hurting me? Why are you criticizing me? Let me be." But if you do not inquire at all, she accuses you of not caring. She lives in an old townhouse near Leicester Square (it belonged to my mother when she left my father and brought us to England). It is the family manse, but still, one has to wonder at the reason. She is near everything, mere blocks from Hammersmith, from the theatre and cafés that she hasn't visited in years. Did she ever? I remember Hermoine as persistently glamorous, I remember chauffeurs and gowns, and late night drinks, and stories of men who flirted with her. That was as far as it went, though. She never – except with one beau, The Count – told me any details that would suggest seduction. But nothing she told me about the men who wanted her suggested that things ever went further than their confessions of desire. That men desired her was inarguable and consequential. It was, she said, an irritant, but when in the clinch (she often used that phrase, 'in the clinch') they couldn't handle her, she was too much for them – too intellectual, too intimidating. One could see that, of course, it was all quite possible. Anything, I suppose, is possible. But then again, of course it's not. What's important is to have relatives, to have Hermoine, because they remind you of your faults. And for me, it's to remind me of my dangerous capacity for dreaming. When I arrived at her flat the lady's maid answered the door. No one these days has a maid, much less a lady's maid. What's amazing about Hermoine's maid is that she's much older and sicker than Hermoine, and can barely walk. I have to ring endlessly as I await her arrival at the door. But bent over as she is, and her frail body wrapped in an old shawl, she manages a crooked, toothless smile. She is happy. This is amazing! She must be in love with Hermoine, or at the very least with the idea of service. She makes her way to the back of the house, for the upstairs bedrooms are not used anymore because neither of them can manage the stairs. So the entire house – our past! – weighs us down like an enormous rock; dark and forbidding. I daren't look up, it might all fall in. I follow her to the back, where Hermoine's room overlooks an overgrown garden – all brown and rumpled – as it is autumn now. The room is disgusting. There is the faintest smell of illness, one isn't quite certain what it is, perhaps a mixture of vomit and excrement. Hermoine sits propped on the bed, managing a wan smile, wearing a thin white slip. Underneath, her aged drooping dugs are vaguely visible. It is time to hug her, I must hug her. All I can think of is John's remark about the old man on the train – "why doesn't he die?" But Hermoine is hanging on; of course it would be out of order to ask why. Hermoine often says, "God must have some reason for keeping me here on earth." Which would be true, of course, if God had reason. I do manage to hug her, or put my head beside hers for a moment, and my hand on her shoulder. Her face seems to be falling off. It is not only the wrinkles, but she has in the past few years been prone to growths, bizarre ones – mostly brown – that stain what was once a lovely face. "So nice to see you," she says. But this descends into a racking cough. I notice now, I don't know why I hadn't noticed before – perhaps because I'm used to seeing these things around her – that there is a lit cigarette on her side table, and a drink as well. Probably vodka. Whatever she has got particularly wrong with her these days – none of this can be good for her. I can't help myself, I have to say it: "Hermoine, are you all right?" A silly question. "It goes, as it goes, as it goes." She shrugs and takes a long puff on her cigarette holder, which causes a brief coughing fit. Again, I can't help myself, "Have you been to see a doctor? She waves me away; this is of course a ridiculous suggestion. "No….No, no. Listen, I know what I want. It's quality, not quantity," she growls. This has been her favourite phrase, ever since she has gotten so terribly sick. The irony is, that she has exactly the opposite. What quality can there be in sitting in bed and slowly drinking herself to death? But it's what she wants. Why? She needs to forget. What is she forgetting? Life? My sister Griselda is outraged by Hermoine's self-neglect. As if reading my mind, Hermoine says, "I was very upset by Griselda yesterday, as I always am. Sometimes I wonder why she comes to visit me if she's just going to yell at me. She demanded I stop drinking. And she told me – this was the strangest thing, chéri – she told me that only last year I had an attack and you had to take me to the hospital. Now I must ask you something, and you must tell me in all honesty; I really can't remember. I can't remember any such thing. Is that true? Did I have an attack? Did I?" This question puts me in a difficult position. On the one hand there is calming Hermoine, which will only happen if I agree with her. On the other hand there is my foolish but persistent attachment to what we call reality. Yes, Hermoine did have an attack, and it was barely six months ago. She called Griselda, and because Hermoine wouldn't go in an ambulance, Griselda's country doctor husband had to transport her to the emergency ward. There she was revived and sent home with pills, which she is probably not taking. So on the one hand there is Aristotelian epistemology – "A is A" – and yes, we did take you to the hospital, Hermoine. But I realize as I look at the wilting, drinking, smoking machine that Hermoine has become, she has simply willed all of this out of her mind. Does it really matter whether or not she really had an attack, if she would rather she hadn't had one, and will not do anything to prevent another one anyway? But I can't stop myself from naming what I see as an occurrence that actually happened. It's all about context. The meaning of an attack in this instance is that it signals Hermoine's confrontation with her own mortality, something which, though she seems wilfully bringing it on, she also most emphatically wishes to avoid. In that sense, in that context, the word 'attack' has no meaning, it does not exist, and it did not happen. "You did have an attack about six months ago," I find myself saying. I don't want to hurt her, but I can't help it. She looks at me oddly – perplexed, shocked, and frightened. If Griselda were to say this, Hermoine would think it cruel. When I say it, it is a reality to be reckoned with. Hermoine, the older sister, has never really liked her younger sister very much, and never trusted her.

She dotes on me; so she is willing to believe my version of events. She says, pitifully, "I wonder why I don't remember." Well of course there are obvious reasons. But I can see that she is afraid she is losing her mind. This fear we certainly don't need, not on top of everything else. "You probably forgot because…because it wasn't important to you. We only remember things that are important to us," I say. This is basically true. "Oh, is that right?" "Yes," I say. "Oh, maybe you're right. But I didn't used to forget things." "I wouldn't worry about it," I say. She takes a drink and in a minute she has forgotten that she was worried about forgetting. I don't stay very much longer; she doesn't want me to. It's important that I be there, but also important that I go. When I step out into the cold clear autumn night I feel very alone. Of course we are all alone. I only feel this way because a meeting with Hermoine is also a meeting with death. When I am seized with longing for Antony the urgency of feeling is due to the romantic notion that thinking of him will make me immortal, that true love will transcend death. It is better to be alone. Truer, colder. Death is, after all, a fact. Of death at least we can be certain. And what of the termination of consciousness? We are sure it happens. But we don't know what it is. It could simply be an alteration, another consciousness. A comforting thought. Or it could just as well be nothing. Not so comforting. But what is nothing? Since we can't describe 'nothing' we act as if it doesn't exist. But the things we can't describe most certainly do exist. That is perhaps something to be certain of, and something which, even if we forget our 'attacks', we must always remember.

Monday 21

I had a student visit me today to talk about his difficulties with his thesis. I am not on his committee, but I am to be admired, looked up to, trusted. When he comes into my office he is cringing and fingering his hat. He wears an orange scarf. Something about him suggests peculiarity, a very specific, studied oddness. He is a thin person who is fat – that is, he has long thin arms and a floppy belly – all out of proportion. "I can't write it because I don't think I can write it," he says, unaware that this is a redundancy. But it is in the second sentence that he reveals what is for him, a fundamental truth. "I'm a neurotic," he says. This is the first time I have ever heard anyone utilize the term in what might be called casual conversation. I cannot say I am entirely pleased about it. "Oh," I say, not the least bit interested in his thesis problems – and why should I be? Since he has clearly stated that he is not capable of writing a thesis, I am happy to take him at his word. But I am also interested in how a person can come to think of himself as a neurotic, and what the empirical effects of such a nominally scientific diagnosis might be. "And how does your neurosis manifest itself?" I say. It's difficult to keep a straight face. But I have convinced him of my earnestness, for he proceeds to unleash a veritable torrent of observations about himself. As I am soon to find out, it is not difficult to persuade a person who considers himself a neurotic to describe his problems and symptoms. Talking about himself and analyzing the mountain of problems that overwhelms him is exactly what a neurotic does best. "I have no self-confidence," he says. "I'm a mess." He says this quite cheerfully; indeed it seems to make him quite happy to say so. "How long have you been lacking in self-confidence?" I ask. "Oh, ever since I was a child. My father was a brute and an idiot." I am shocked by the candidness of this disclosure. But this, again, will prove to be typical of such a personality. "Was he a clinical idiot?" I ask. "What do you mean?" asks The Neurotic. "I mean, was he mentally retarded?" "Oh, no," he says, smiling again, "I just meant he was an idiotic person. He spanked me brutally and criticized me as a child and did not give me the support that I needed or deserved." "And what kind of support was that?" I asked. "Well, all children need the support of their fathers. All boys wish to be their fathers, and lie with their mothers." This is a somewhat too literal reading of Freud, but I let it pass. I do not want to appear too critical. "And you find that this lack of self-confidence has made it difficult for you to work on your thesis?" "Oh yes," he says. "Every time I approach my typewriter I feel a chill. It's as if I am freezing to death." "Perhaps you have left the window open," I say, and immediately feel guilty. Honestly I did not mean to make fun of him. But this addled creature, who claims he lacks any form of self-confidence, is surprisingly articulate in his own defence. "I would ask you not to make fun of me, sir, for that attitude will further encourage my doubts." As his orange scarf has fallen, he takes the opportunity to whip it over his shoulder, again in a paradoxically rakish and self-confident gesture. "I have come to see you because your learning is deep, and your wisdom world-renowned, and I would appreciate it if you could help me. If you are critical of me I may very well become a victim of transference." I asked him if he might define what he means by that. "If you are abusive to me, I will transfer my resentment of my idiot father onto you." I resist the urge to remind him that persistently calling his father an idiot – rather than idiotic – might lead people to assume that he is descended from a mental deficient, but quickly realize that comments like these would be seen as criticism, and lead to further transference and loss of self-esteem. I also realize that it is, in fact, impossible to talk to a neurotic. It is far easier to listen. This results, I think, from the fact that authentic Freudian psychoanalysis requires the patient to visit the doctor for an hour every day, and it is tempting for the psychoanalytic patient to demand similar obeisance from his family and friends. "I did not mean to be abusive," I say. "I accept your apology," says The Neurotic. "But how am I to gain the self-confidence to write my thesis?" "Well," I say, surprised at myself for going out on a limb, "You must simply make the decision to be self-confident." "That sounds deceptively simple," he says. "It is," I say. "But you can't just make a decision to be self-confident; if you could, then everybody would walk around being self-confident all the time." "But most people do that," I say. "No, most people are, deep down, paralyzed with fears they have inherited from their dramatic, primal, family scene." At this point, I am speechless, which is rare, for me. I dare not try and give him a solution, I dare not dismiss his concerns, and I certainly dare not ask him to leave my office, as this is liable to hurt his feelings. I realize another fundamental truth about dealing with a neurotic. One must become more neurotic than they are. "I'm sorry," I say, "but I am becoming paralyzed by my inability to help you. It is making me feel very insecure." "I'm sorry," says The Neurotic. My ruse has worked. We are now speaking the same language. "Is it better that I leave you alone?" he asks. "Leave me alone with my self doubt," I say. "I'm sorry if I caused your insecurity," he says. "No, no," I say blithely, "it is always there." "What a surprise that a famous philosopher like yourself is insecure," he says. "Please don't tell anyone," I say. "It will only make me more insecure." "I understand," says The Neurotic, rising to a standing position. "Well, thanks for listening to me." He looks at me awkwardly, and then throws his orange scarf – which has once more fallen down – over his shoulder. I can see that he is resisting the urge to cry. Instead, he simply edges out of the room, thanking me profusely. He leaves me overawed by the wonder of Freudian science. I am astounded by his faith in it, which, like our faith in all matters scientific, is beyond question, and quite literally, beyond belief.

Saturday 26

I have not written in this journal for many days because I have been deeply engaged with designing the house for my sister. Today I presented her and her husband with the plans. I am still reeling. Not from their response. No, I am reeling from my own audacity and from suspicions about my own motives. How can we not know why we do things? And yet it is certainly one of the most common feelings in the world. The murderer cries, "Why oh why did I kill her; I loved her and now she is gone." The psychiatrist is right at hand, ready to analyze. But actions are not motives, they are simply actions, and it is a language game which would lead us to believe that they must have a necessary interiority. On the other hand, it's hard for me to believe that my actions are innocent. I love my sister, I know that I do. I wanted to design them a house. I have presented them with the initial plans. The plans may or may not be suitable for them. It is up to them to decide. They must take responsibility for their decision. What I am feeling is guilt. This is not rational. I have done nothing wrong. I am merely designing a house – one that I think will be the best house in the world. But will it be the best house for them? Certainly I designed it specifically with them in mind. But they are the epitome of normalcy, so a house for them is a house for the world. The house is not comfortable, because it is not always wise to be comfortable. Or rather, the idea of a comfort is a contradiction in terms. For comfort initiates within us the need for more of comfort;

comfort is a drug. This is why there would be no cushions anywhere. (Not in the traditional sense of cushions.) First of all, I noticed that my sister's family is quite well padded on their posteriors. Nature made them that way so that there would be no need to spend money on extra cushions. This is not to say that I am demanding that there be no cushions on the chairs, or mattresses on the beds. I see the furniture as square; it is very important that it be square, and flat, and spare, and unpainted. There will be no paint anywhere, and the house will be made of wood, and all the joints on all the beams will be visible. It will be like living in a tree house, or in the branches of a tree, or in a construction site. The house will not appear to be finished – because finishing is false – an illusion, a facade. So the wooden chairs must be padded with something. But not cushions. Not the lying obscenity of a cushion, which is to cover the wood and deny it. No. A pad, a simple pad, which is blonde in colour, the colour of the wood. It lies there as a concession to the need for the smallest bit of comfort, without which we cannot rest and cannot sleep. I discussed both the pads, and the furniture, immediately, even before we got to the design of the rooms. This I found disconcerting, putting the cart before the horse. But I had brought a sample pad along with me that attracted their attention, and they demanded I explain the whole principle of lack of adornment. It was at this point that I became initially concerned, and somewhat disappointed by their reaction. I began to see what would be typical of our afternoon – that I would present an idea with enthusiasm, and they would receive it with eagerness, until it became very clear what I was proposing, and then the eagerness would wane, and the eyes of the couple would meet. The country doctor would hug his wife, and she would smile, and toss her ringlets, and they would reassure me that I was a genius and that genius just takes some understanding – especially since the two of them are emphatically not geniuses. I think all this talk of geniuses is foolish, and I say so. I am excited to tell them more, and so we move on. And it seems at first that they have dismissed their disappointment and/or confusion, and are no longer concerned that there will be no over-padded cushions in their new home. Really, if I had to explain my concerns over the notion of 'comfort' it would all be about the war, or it would be about the months that I spent in Norway, or probably – and this is insanity in its own way – it would be about Antony. And what about all those who don't have hugs, or food, or movies, or drinking or cushions, or Antony? How unjust is it for us to revel in ours when they have none! How Lutheran I sound. No. It really is much more a matter of this: we must not try and make the world something that it is not, for this can only lead to disappointment. Think of the children, I would have said – if they had asked me to explain the philosophical implications of my house. Should they grow up in a world where all is ordered and comfortable and sweet and loving? For this is not the way the world is in actuality. It seems to me that the neurosis which occupies so many these days has less to do with some trauma initiated by our imperfect parents, than with the simple universal trauma of discovering that the world is not as our mothers told us. At any rate my sister and her husband come to accept the idea of pads instead of cushions, and of square furniture. And then I move on to the idea that the house should be filled, in effect, with optical illusions, or perhaps what would be more accurate to say – logical illusions. That is, I did not intend the house to be actually dangerous; booby-trapped. I did not want the house to hurt them, or hurt the children, or be a place that they would have difficulty moving about in. On the other hand, I can see no sense in building a house founded on the conviction that life makes sense. Logic is ultimately illogical when we try and apply it to the real world. Just as it makes no sense for the children to have an overly comfortable house, it also makes no sense for them to have a house that assures them that the world is a pleasing, well structured, logical place, where one thing follows another in orderly sequence, and everything has a cause as well as an effect. How much wiser these children will become, maturing in a house which teaches them that life is unexpected, unexplained, confusing, infuriating, devilish – grimly, starkly, unbendingly strange. It is important for me that none of the rooms be square. This I think will be an odd contrast with the furniture, which is square, and gives the feeling that life itself involves being a square peg in a round hole. But by that I do not mean to suggest that the rooms would be round, but rather that they would be multisided, and irregular. It is also important that there be many closets. Closets are necessary to put things in, and because they are secret places, and secrets are important too. Everyone has secrets, and to deny we have them is to lie, or perhaps to live in a Freudian fantasy where we can at all times reveal everything about ourselves. If a closet is to remain a secret then it must not announce itself. And how does a door announce itself? With a handle. Why need a door have a handle? Handles are invariably ugly and occasions for nightmarish orgies of decoration, of *baroquery* and mannerism, of grotesque *roccoesque* excess. A door can be pushed in, a door can be pressed upon and it will open, if it is on a kind of spring. I imagine walls that are seamless and flat and uniform, except of course for the fact that they are all at oddly different angles. And what of windows? Well they, too, should be hidden, until they are needed. A switch could be pressed and a wall could slide and a window could appear. Why? What is the necessity for this nonsense? Because I think a room should be *tabula rasa*. It should not be imposed upon by the designer. It should be nothing. This is as the universe is, until man enters and seeks, in his audacity and his conceit, to imprint his soul upon it. This means that each person, when they enter the room, will also feel that there is nothing in it, that there are just square chairs and square beds with the lean pads on them, and nothing on the walls, no decoration, no windows or doors. Just walls at odd angles. It is up to the person who lives in that room to make of it what they will, which is exactly what happens in life. It is up to us to impose our will – through language – on reality, which offers us nothing, or at least would seem to offer us nothing, if we had not decided to name it, categorize it, list it, organize it, etc. There was an excitement when I explained this idea to Griselda and her husband. But when I moved on to the final idea I saw fear. And this frightened me. It wasn't blatant fear, as with an animal on the road about to be hit by an oncoming car. It was more a kind of sadness mixed with disappointment – indicated by a slightly furrowed brow. I told them finally that each room should have something in it that was fundamentally wrong. Or more clearly, each room must have something fundamentally wrong with it. And by this I mean, as I explained to them, that each room should have something perplexing about it, something which makes one uncomfortable and confused. Of course this confusion and perplexity would pass. But the initial reaction to the room would always be in one's memory. And part of one's love for it would be this oddness, this bold illogic, this mistake. When I said the word mistake their brows furrowed visibly, both of them, and I thought that they might demur. I told them of course that my feelings would not be in any way hurt if they decided not to build the house that I so wished to build for them. But I also told them I would be happier to have them reject the house completely and build their own fantasy house, than to have them ask me to build the house in a way which partially realized my vision, or realized some aspects of it but not others. No, upon thinking about this, upon writing this, I can see that I have done nothing wrong. Yes, I have envisioned for them a challenging house, perhaps a frightening one, and it will require them to think and solve problems and create. But I don't think that's such an awful thing, I think it is a gift. I left them thinking, I could tell that they were thinking. But they were also very excited. Well, we'll see what our next meeting will bring.

Monday 28

The oddest evening with Arthur. I must write it down. I don't understand it. He has had the queerest effect on me. I probably shouldn't think about it. It's clear to me that Arthur's judgement is affected by emotion, and he reacts to films before he even has a chance to think about them, if he thinks about them at all. But he said something to me that upset me very much. I think it was unkind. There is, of course, no unkindness where logic is concerned. An observation is just an observation, and if it is hurtful then that is simply the result – an unintentional result perhaps – of an unhappy accident. If one sets out to hurt, that is a different matter. Did he set out to hurt me? I think he may have, and I think that this is another reason not to see him again. In fact the situation has grown into one of those where it may be necessary to finally decide whether or not I see Arthur again. I don't like having to make such decisions. It would be better if he simply went away. Perhaps if I treat him badly, ignore him, etc., he will go away. He seems like the sensitive type. But then again perhaps he is not, since he hurt me so gratuitously, with such ease. Here I am again with the question of motive, and I am thinking suspiciously like a Freudian. What should it matter what his motives were? I was late; it was horrible for me to be late. It was raining, and cold. It's the kind of rain that is becoming a wintery rain, very inhospitable. I had been at a faculty meeting. I never go to them if it is at all humanly possible. It is quite possible for the discussion to get down to the placement of a period in an administrative edict. Literally. I have seen it happen. There is one professor, Professor Witmore – to myself I sometimes call him 'Professor Kafka' – who has that rarest of talents, to bring an afternoon to a full stop. Whether or not time comes to a stop on a train moving at the speed of light, it certainly comes to a stop at a meeting when Witmore decides to argue a minute point. Today he decided to take issue with the fact that a course on 19th Century Philosophy had the word 'between' in it. The course was to be entitled "Between Nietzche and Logical Positivism, a Critique of Post Enlightenment Thought." Admittedly the word 'between' is, in this case, inaccurate. But this is where Witmore and I would differ. To me, it is a matter of acute indifference whether or not a course title is accurate or not. It seems lovely, even poetic, that an inconsequential preposition like 'between' can offer such a wealth of resonances and spark a lively discussion. But not for Witmore. For him the word 'between' is dangerous because it is not the right word. What follows is a long discussion about what the right word might be. It finally gets to the point where Witmore forces a vote. The phrase which he has chosen to replace 'between' is – 'at the interjunction of'. This is rejected, because as far as anyone knows there is no such word as 'interjunction', and even if there is, and it means, as Witmore suggests, an intersection between two things, what possible 'interjunction' is there between Nietzche and Comte? But at this point it has become a personal matter for Professor Witmore. Indeed we begin to think it is going to have an adverse affect on his health if the vote does not go his way. He leads a kind of filibuster against the word 'between' in which there is, on Witmore's part, much banging on tables, sweating, prancing about and shaking of his gleaming, bald head. Finally the department wisely decides to take his suggestion – but only after this very tedious and frustrating meeting has run nearly an hour late. Thankfully, I am not an hour late for Arthur, yet I am nonetheless late, and it is raining and cold, and I think that I am going to get pneumonia. I can see that Arthur is frustrated too, even though he doesn't express it. And of course he is wet, so we rush into the theatre. No one is there because it is a Monday. An empty old theatre is a sinister thing. Apparently the movie is a flop. It's called, *Bringing Up Baby,* and Arthur just has to see it because it features Katherine Hepburn, of whom he is inordinately fond. I have never heard of her. But he assures me that the film will be much more to my taste than *Grand Hotel,* because it is what he calls a 'madcap comedy'. The idea of madcap comedy is certainly appealing to me, and I am hoping that there will be dance numbers featuring aerial photography. Arthur insists on the balcony. I don't know why; it is even lonelier up there except for a forlorn and very slender young usher with a flashlight – he is slender in an unhealthy way – who leads us to our seats. There appear to be only two other people in the theatre, an unlucky couple who have also ventured out on a cold and rainy night to see a movie that no one else wants to see. When we look down on them they are closely cuddled, which suggests that movie watching is probably the least of their concerns. We settle in and I am soon even more bored than I was with *Grand Hotel.* In this movie everything is unlikely and the characters talk too fast. This film in no way resembles the way people talk or act in what we know as real life. Both Katherine Hepburn and Cary Grant are very beautiful, and one thinks they might be very adept at something else – but not this. The situation is also unlikely – Cary Grant plays an absent-minded palaeontologist who is trying to put together a dinosaur and marry his fiancée when he is suddenly interrupted by Katherine Hepburn, who talks incomprehensible nonsense at breakneck speed. I found two things endearing, but hardly endearing enough to rescue the film for me. Early in the film Katherine Hepburn wears a dress which is unlikely but beautiful. Attached to the dress is a cape made of cellophane that hovers over her shoulders like the wings of an angel. Later, she brings home a pet leopard – the explanation for the appearance of this leopard strained the limits of earthly logic to say the least – and the only way she can keep the leopard calm is to sing a song called "I can't give you anything but love, baby." This is a very sweet song, made even sweeter by its nonsensicalness. But the song is contradictory, because though it has a pretty tune, it posits a highly undesirable situation. Why would a person ever want to be with someone who could *only* give them love? I think Arthur must have known how bored I was, because I crossed and uncrossed my legs many times. When the lights came up the couple below were gone. They must have been bored too, or more likely simply had better things to do. There was an awkward moment where we stood up and stretched. And then Arthur suggested we go to a tearoom. I was not in the mood for tea, but his question was hopeful and I didn't want to hurt his feelings. When we left the theatre the rain had stopped, but it was a still breezy, so I was thankful that the tearoom was only a few doors away. A nice old woman served us, and the furniture resembled the ugly, comforting kind one might find in a grandmother's house. We sat opposite each other in awkward silence punctuated only by Arthur's comments about the passers-by on the street. Then, finally, Arthur asked me if I liked the movie. I saw no point in lying. He looked disappointed, but took a breath and asked

"Why?" I told him that the movie was completely unlikely. He told me that was a contradiction, because in a lecture on aesthetics I had once said that what made films interesting was their unlikeliness. This was absolutely true, and I was surprised by his perspicuity. I explained that the kind of movies that I had praised in class were the kind of films that are my favourites – musical comedies – and that they are set in another fantasy universe and have no relationship to reality whatsoever. These films don't ask us to believe that they are real. A movie such as *Bringing Up Baby*, on the other hand, seems to take place in the reality that we know. Thus, when it strays too far from the realm of the known it strikes us as silly. "What about when she cried?" he asked. I could not remember a moment when Katherine Hepburn cried. "Did you fall asleep?" he asked, with an incredulous smile. I told him that I did not. When he described the moment when she cried, I remembered it. But I did not remember that she cried, only that she was sad. Apparently she said to Cary Grant, "I will always love you no matter what," and, "Everything I do with the best intentions turns out badly." Arthur thought that these lines were pitiful and they moved him. I pointed out that both statements were logical fallacies. The first statement, "I will always love you no matter what," refers to a kind of love that makes no sense whatsoever. "What if for instance, you were to love someone and they were to commit a murder. Would you still love them?" I asked him. "But I could never love someone who was capable of murder," said Arthur. I did not see how Arthur could be certain of this, and said so. "Because I could never love a truly bad person," he said. This seemed to me sentimental, not logical. I thought it best not to pursue it and went on to the next bit of dialogue. "'Everything I do with the best intentions turns out badly' is a false paradox," I told him. "It assumes that intentions are intrinsically related to their results. This is not true." I could see that he was growing weary of my logic, which disappointed me. But I felt sorry for him, so I mentioned a moment of the film that rang true for me. It had a kind of anti-logic. There is a moment when Cary Grant puts on a woman's dressing gown, and an older woman comes to the door, and she asks him what he is doing. He says, "I'm sitting in the middle of a street waiting for a bus." This moment was not actually funny, but it was interesting, because it suggests that words might sometimes mean something very different from what they are supposed to. What if 'Sitting on a curb' actually meant, 'Standing in a dress'? I also told him that it struck me as interesting that Cary Grant's character – perhaps due to his uncomfortableness about wearing a dress – actually seemed to believe for a moment that he was in another place. After I delivered this little speech there was a pause, and I decided to pour myself some more tea. I looked at Arthur and he looked back at me with a strange intensity, as if I had just hit him. I noticed particularly how dark his eyes were and how they matched his thin, youthful beard. "Do you mind if I make an observation?" he asked carefully. I told him of course not. "A personal observation?" he asked. I told him I couldn't see why not. He took a breath and leaned back, placing one hand on the table, and with the other hand he carefully pointed at me. "You remind me very much of the character that Cary Grant played in the movie." I must say I was shocked. "But that character, that character was ridiculous." "I'm not saying you're ridiculous," he said. "I didn't make a value judgement," he added. "But that character is so absent-minded that he forgets that he is supposed to be married," I said. "Yes," said Arthur, staring at me in a challenging, unwavering way. "Well I am flabbergasted," I said. "Do you really imagine that I am so separated from the day to day routine of things?" "Yes," he said firmly, staring at me. I was astounded by this. Not so much by his assertion. I am sure it had some truth to it. I am, after all a professor, and so busy thinking most of the time that I am probably quite unrelated to day to day events. No, what astounded me was his persistence, even in the face of my shock, which must have been intimidating for him. I saw him clear his throat and gather his courage. "Do you know how long your pauses are?" he asked. "My pauses?" I said. "Yes," he said. "What pauses?" I asked. "The pauses you make in your lectures," he said. Well of course I knew what he was talking about, I am quite aware that I pause quite frequently during the lectures; I'm not completely insane. I told him that, yes, I was quite aware of the pauses. "But do you know how long they are?" he asked. "Oh, a few seconds or so I would assume," I said. "No," he said, staring at me, shaking his head. "Well, how long then?" "You once took a pause that lasted for three minutes." "Three minutes!" I couldn't believe this. "That's not possible." "I didn't think so, but I checked my watch." "No, I don't believe you." "Well, it's true." "Is it?" "Of course it is. Why would I lie?" I looked at him, he seemed almost triumphant, as he leaned back in his little wooden chair. Indeed I could think of no good reason. It was at this point that something happened. I was seized with an emotion, and it was not a pleasant one. It was fear. I do not often feel fear; I do not like to feel it. I resented this young man very much for bringing on that feeling. "Why did you say that to me?" I said. "Because it's true," he said. "I thought you might be interested." "Well I'm not," I said. "Will you excuse me?" I asked, "I have to go to the bathroom." When I got inside I shut the door. I looked in the mirror. I noticed that I looked particularly shabby that day. I also noticed that my left eyebrow had grown rather long. I'm at that age when the eyebrows begin to grow uncontrollably. And then, the realization both that I was in possession of an eyebrow with an almost comic furriness and that I had – at least in one instance – taken a pedagogical pause long enough for students to cook an egg in, made me very anxious indeed. It seemed possible to me, for a moment, that I was going mad. I thought of walking right out of the tearoom without speaking to Arthur but this would have been too melodramatic. What I was feeling was beyond melodrama. Suddenly there was a knock on the door. This was very odd. The door to the bathroom did not lock. It was spacious, with two stalls. Why would someone knock? I said, "Yes?" The door opened. It was Arthur. "May I come in?" he asked. I was incapable of speaking. He came in and stood beside me. We both stood in front of the mirror. I noticed that, though Arthur was only about fifteen years younger than me, he looked young enough to be my grandson. I felt like a foolish old man, and I wanted him to go away. "I'm sorry," he said. "There's nothing to be sorry for," I said. "You simply stated a fact. If it is true." "I didn't mean to upset you," he said. Then he did the oddest thing. In a very sweet and proprietary way, he kissed my cheek. Again, I was flabbergasted. "I was very concerned about you," he said. "Sometimes you just seem so distant from things." I looked down at the floor, not at him. "And necessarily so. Listen, I think you'd better leave me alone for awhile." "What do you mean?" he asked. "I think I'd better go home," I said. And with that, I pushed past him and walked out of the tearoom. There was really nothing he could do, because we hadn't paid the bill. I saw him paying it as I crossed in front of the window, but it was no use; he would not catch me. I disappeared around a corner, and anyway, he has no idea where I live. I went directly home and wrote this. I am now putting this away and going to bed. I can't think of any possible motive for Arthur saying what he said. But the more I think about it, the more difficulty I think I will have sleeping, so it's best now for me to stop all this and go to bed.

Tuesday 29

It was an extraordinary morning. Not a happy one. Two things happened. I could not stop thinking of Antony and I had a not very pleasant encounter with Nigel. The first thing was definitely precipitated by my encounter, last night, with Arthur, the second was felicitous chance. All morning I was supposed to be correcting papers. But this morning, try as I might, I could not settle down to work. I could think only of Antony, and all in comparison to Arthur. It was suddenly clear to me why the thinking of Antony had been coming in such waves of despair and intensity. I had, somewhere, at the back of my mind – because of the torn pocket – imagined that Arthur was a person in my life who could replace Antony. It was suddenly so obvious, and so pitiful, that I wanted to kick myself. No one had really shown an interest in me since Antony and here was Arthur inquiring if I wanted to see a movie, so of course I would project onto him some of my feelings for Antony. But Arthur was not Antony and never would be. Never would Antony have reproached me, never would he have criticized me or suggested that I was not connected with whatever Arthur felt that I was not connected with. In fact, of the two of us, Antony was definitely least connected to 'things'. It was Antony who had the unrealistic fancies and plans, it was Antony who suggested climbing mountains, staying out all night in the dangerous woods. It was Antony who wanted to spend hours musing and arguing with no thought to how he might earn a living or exist from day to day. Antony was like me, a thinker, an independent; he challenged me, he pushed me further, he made me move further along towards the best of myself by setting an example. The affection we had was unstated because it had to be. He could not have been physically affectionate with anyone, I do not think he could bear it. He never, ever would have kissed me, like Arthur. But Antony did not need to kiss me; it would have been like kissing a mirror. It was idiotic to compare Antony and Arthur. It was like two different languages – two different realities. The reality of Antony was gone, and would never be in my life again. Arthur was here, and obviously trying to push his way into my life. But it wasn't to happen because we were just too phenomenally different. And when it came down to it Arthur was just not terribly smart. How could he not recognize the ridiculousness of a phrase like "I will love you no matter what?" I thought in this manner all morning, did not work, and decided there was no point in thinking about it any longer and would have to stop. When I thought I could push these ideas around no more there was a knock on my office door. It was Nigel. He had his usual rosy chubby red-cheeked look. His nose, however, was a little too red. (I often wonder, does he drink?) He asked if he could sit down for a moment and I told him that it was no problem, only because I frankly hoped he would divert my mind in another direction. I asked him why he had come, and he said: "Oh, cultural relativity and cognitive relativity of course." This was not an 'of course' to me. I had forgotten, first of all, that he wanted to talk with me about these topics, and anyway had harboured the hope from the start that we might never have to. He has a couple of axes to grind in this area; he is essentially conservative and unadventurous in his thinking. There is always a certain point, with Nigel, when, after arguing a topic for a while, he simply looks at you in a very unscholarly way – the way one bloke might look at another bloke – and says: "Come now, seriously, do you really believe that?" This is an argument from intimidation. All one can really do is say, firmly, "Yes, in fact, I do." This brings the conversation to a stop. But after that Nigel gives you the feeling you have betrayed him and are bluffing. A conversation about anything could only end in this, so why bother? But now he was here, and had started, and there was nothing I could do. "I have no problem with cultural relativity," he said. He seemed to think this would make me happy. I couldn't have cared less. Then he went on to expound on the manner in which different cultures find that they are incomprehensible to each other, and how customs of marriage in, say, Cameroon are different from our own. And then he hit on a key point of contention: "Of course it is quite possible for one culture to understand the differences of another, for, even if they do not share a common language, they can find a way to communicate as a point of reference." I agreed with him on this: of course we could through sign language with a Cameroonian, somehow communicate. "Well, here is where I have a problem with cognitive relativity," he said. "How can it be possible that we have no point of reference with another form of cognition?" Well, I think it is possible, and I told him so. "But how can that be?" he asked. I told him that it was something that was very difficult to prove, as of course, we may in fact have no way of thinking about people whose perceptions and language are so very different from ours. Depending on how different from us they might be, we might not even know they exist at all. I was simply talking off the top of my head. He looked at me, flatly: "You don't really believe that there are people in the world somewhere who think about things in ways that we will never understand? Do you? Really?" He had perfected the argument of intimidation; never had I seen him look quite so candidly shocked, and so ready and able to find a common ground on which, of course, I would be expected to surrender. "Yes, I do." "Not really?" He asked again. "Yes I do," I said, "And I think that until you are ready to bring an actual argument to the table, there is no point at all in us talking about this any further." I didn't want to insult him, but I could see no other way of getting him out of my office. "Well," he said, "I just wondered." The implication being that I was melodramatic in the extreme. In the realm of ideas, I am quite simply the opposite.

Wednesday 30

Another bad day. It began with The Neurotic. My fatal mistake has been being nice to him. It is always my fatal mistake. It is most certainly my fatal mistake with Arthur. I feel sorry for these students and then I am civil to them and they hang about like dogs. So, because I did not sufficiently humiliate The Neurotic he is back sitting opposite me in that infuriating way, looking fat and thin at the same time, and wallowing in his self confessed inability to manage his life. I wish I shared Nigel's joy in treating the students like dirt. I suppose I see myself in some of them, those who are shabby-looking adolescents; they will, in the future, become shabby adults. He didn't waste any time. He told me that his problem was me, an obsession with me – I was so productive, I was so brilliant, I had changed the world of philosophy, I had done this and I had done that. It's true that I have published a book that people still talk about, but I told him that it was a very small book and that I didn't like it any more. He was taken aback, to an alarming degree. "You don't like your own book!" he exclaimed. "How can that be!" "Well, I think I was mistaken," I told him. "But how?" "I theorized that logic has some relationship to reality, but of course it doesn't. Today I wonder how I could ever have been so stupid." "That must be very difficult for you to endure," he said. I was suddenly fascinated by his manner of speaking. It occurred to me that perhaps it was this way of talking that made him feel things so melodramatically rather than the other way around. I told him that it was not difficult to change one's scholarly approach; it was challenging, even invigorating, and that trying to understand the relationship between reality and logic had been the focus of my research ever since. "You're so purposeful, always directed towards a goal," said The Neurotic, "whereas I do nothing." I decided to challenge this linguistic hyperbole. "You do nothing?" "Absolutely nothing!" he pronounced, mournfully, taking his head in his gloved hand. I noticed he was wearing purple gloves, which I thought was most certainly, in its own way, doing something. "Tell me what you did yesterday," I demanded. "Nothing," he said. "You can't possibly have done nothing. You'd be dead if you did absolutely nothing. You must have gotten up, eaten breakfast." "Yes, I did that." Yes, hence the fat/thin look. "And what else?" I asked. "I tell you – nothing." "What kind of nothing?" I persisted. "I sat and looked at the garden," he said. Let me ask you a question," I said. "Yes?" he looked hopeful. "Have you ever heard the phrase 'you must take the time to smell the roses'?" I presumed he had heard of it. It was a typical English expression. "There are so many people in this world who are unable to do that, who cannot take time to smell the roses. You, however, can. You did. Yesterday." "I don't know what you mean," he said. It occurred to me that perhaps the reason he couldn't write his paper was because he was, quite simply, stupid. "You have perfected the art of doing nothing. Of living. Not filling it with unnecessary activity – just letting yourself be. Maybe that is your gift." I was able to put some actual emotion into this, because I wanted to help him, but also because it is something that I believe. And I am always amazed at the power of belief to change people's perceptions of the world. He stood up behind the chair, lightly grazing the back of it with his gloved hand. "What you've just said is very profound," he said. It was also a commonplace, but I hesitated to mention that, as the commonplace was working its usual magic. And I was praying that this awe might motivate him to leave my office. It did. He wandered thoughtfully over to the door, thanked me, and after a longing look in my direction, he left. After this encounter, I had an interminable class. I couldn't concentrate properly, which forced me to make an apology to the students. This is very much due to Arthur, who, by the way, didn't attend class that day. It was impossible for me to think – all because he had mentioned the length of my pauses. Every time I stopped talking all I could think about was how long I had been thinking. This meant that I had nothing terribly interesting to say. When I left the class my thoughts were only of John. In fact I had never felt quite the same urge to see him. I walked directly to the train station. I did not take off my tie, I merely loosened it. As usual I had no idea if he would be there. Sure enough, when I arrived at the station, I saw him standing leaning on a pole, talking with someone. It was my guess that it would be a girl. Predictably, she was young and pretty, the type that he liked. She seemed very interested in him, and why shouldn't she be? I watched them for a few minutes, with pleasure. I was not jealous. There was nothing for me to be jealous of. It was in fact John's pleasure in the world that gave me, in turn, pleasure. The girl did enjoy the same thing about him, I was sure of that, too. We had something in common: our love of life itself, through John. After a moment or two, he saw me. I didn't try and catch his eye, I was merely watching them. He proffered a glance at me in a way that suggested acknowledgement. He said something funny to her that made her throw her head back and laugh, and then he was away. He walked over to me in that way he has, very cocky, very proud of himself. He leaned over to me, confidentially, "She's quite the looker, eh, mate?" Yes I had to admit she was. "Look at the titties on her!" He said dangerously, for she was in hearing distance. The girl looked as if she had just remembered something, and walked away. "Whew, I hope she didn't hear me. I mean I hope she did." He chucked me under the rib with his elbow. The feeling was not at all unpleasant. I simply said, "Come here." "What is it, mate?" "Come along," I said, not inhospitably. I walked towards the train station bathroom. He followed me obediently, his interest piqued. I usually let him take the lead. Here was something different. John was always up for something different. When we arrived at the bathroom we found what I was looking for. A mirror. A mirror like in the tearoom. I stood in front of the mirror and examined the two of us. Then I took his hand. He was roughly the same age as Arthur – somewhere around thirty years old – but when I stood looking at myself in the mirror with him he didn't look inappropriately youthful, I didn't look like his grandfather. I noticed that, infuriatingly, my eyebrow still looked too long. I grabbed him and kissed him full on the mouth. He was not unpleasantly surprised. "Whoah mate!" he said. I pushed him against the wall and pressed myself on top of him. He put up a mock fight. This time he didn't seem to want to win. We struggled together like a mockery of two prizefighters, only this time wrapped in an erotic embrace. Time stopped. When I was finished I drew away from him. He looked at me sheepishly. It occurred to me that someone could easily have come in and found us. But what would they have seen? Two friends wrestling. A younger one – and an older one with a bushy eyebrow. Was that a cause for concern? John looked at me in the mirror with admiration, as he washed his hands. "I didn't know you had it in you, mate."

Well, frankly, I didn't know it either. I washed my hands too. It seemed like the correct thing to do. He was still agog. "I got to watch out for you mate, next thing you know you'll be slipping me one." This was much cause for laughter. I couldn't help myself. I laughed too. At this point a man entered the bathroom. He looked like a prosperous businessperson; he was well dressed and carried a suitcase. He didn't seem to approve of this laughter in bathrooms. I couldn't say whether I approved of it either. All I knew was that in my desperation I had forgotten time for a moment again, and it had brought me a kind of relief. John and I clapped each other on the back after we left the bathroom, and went our separate ways.

Friday 2

Thursday was a wreck, I couldn't work. My brother had been weighing on my mind. I decided it was time to visit him. When I called him, he answered the phone in that distracted way he has, searching for focus – "Yes, um, just a second yes, you here. Hmm. Yes. I would very much like to have you here. Take the next train." He is always succinct, precise and direct; one of the few things I love about him. I can't say why I needed to see him, I just did. Going to visit my brother always brings things to a head; he is like myself – only concentrated, exaggerated, in a fun house mirror. If something must change in my life, going to see my brother will always precipitate it. He is like a good tonic, a psychic purging. Madness does that – there is no possibility of compromise. I was still obsessed with the extravagant growth on my eyebrow, so I went to the train station and picked up a ticket – my brother lives in Cornwall, of all places – which left me enough time to go to the barber and have my eyebrow trimmed. The barber was an irritating fellow. I don't know why I keep returning to him. Yes I do, his shop is convenient. He would not merely trim my eyebrow, even though I offered to pay him the price of a full haircut for it. No, he must have noticed my shabbiness, he insisted on cutting my hair. There was time for it, and he was very persistent, so I let him. I wanted to kill him. I don't like haircuts, abhor a stranger touching my head. It seems such a private place. Which of course I understand, it is not. It is painfully evident to me that there is nothing being carried in my head which is not being carried in the head of any person of intelligence, as we all think about things in basically the same way. On the other hand, a person like The Neurotic seems almost cognitively inhibited, neurally impaired by his melodramatic way of expressing himself. This suggests to me that he does, in a way, speak another language. Language makes us all the same but it also makes us different. It is a paradox. But at any rate I don't like people touching my head. And then there were his filthy instruments. This barber does not clean his tools; this I do not understand, there is no excuse for him not having an immaculate workplace. And on top of that he takes such a dreadfully long time. He considers himself an artist. No, a scientist, that's what he is, a scientist of hair. I am not denigrating his profession. It is perhaps even a craft. But the endless tweaking, standing back, and looking in the mirror. Why do we scientists take so much pride in what we do? It is the cause of so much bad work. He even has the white coat, the uniform of the scientist, the expert, the saint who dispenses wisdom. Finally he is finished and I hurl the money into his hand and run towards my train. It is a beautiful trip; it always is. It was a wild day at the end of autumn. And as you approach Cornwall the landscape gets wilder and wilder, until you can smell the sea in the air, and erratic breezes which rearrange everything. The trees, which had a 17th century Dutch delicacy about them, were being lashed by the wind in such a way that it seemed to me that a tornado might be attacking the English countryside. I am not used to the sea. My brother's house, to all intents and purposes, is on a cliff. It is a dilapidated old estate that he purchased many years ago. He lives there by himself. He can't keep servants. He abuses them mercilessly, changes his mind, and makes extravagant orders.

He must have two cases of wine, must have them now, they must be a certain kind of wine – something special, foreign, old, and unavailable. And if he cannot get what he wants, he has a fit, hurls things about. So instead of servants he gets his students – because he teaches piano – to come and clean house for him occasionally. His students are devoted to him – much in the way my students are to me – but it is altogether different. He is a bad influence. He really shouldn't be around adolescents, they are so impressionable. And it is quite clear to me that he enjoys ordering them around. He has never told me so outright; these are things we wouldn't talk about, human relationships are generally too petty and demeaning to concern my brother, but it is evident. Many a time I have come to visit him and seen some poor boy or girl scrubbing the floor or beating the rugs and glancing at my brother with an adoration more appropriate for stage or screen idols. As I disembarked from the train and entered the taxi I prepared myself for the inevitable drama; my brother would have discovered something, would be in the midst of a revelation, an epiphany. I have never known him not to be. Entering his house is like entering the eye of a hurricane. I pay the cabbie and knock on the door. There is even a knocker; it is like something out of Dickens or Jane Eyre. For a moment I imagine myself to be an innocent governess. My brother opens the door. For some reason he is wearing riding boots, jodhpurs and a white nightshift, with long billowing sleeves. It is an outrageous getup but of course I don't expect an explanation. I know if I ask he will wave his hand: "It's very complicated… not important!" So I don't. He bows, as far as he can bow, in the cramped, baroque vestibule. "You are here." And in this way he confirms my presentness, the idea of me being present, and inside this very moment with him. But what he really means to do is be cordial, in fact overwhelmed. "My little brother is here. My only brother." The fact that he raises that issue so early in the meeting does not bode well. I am his only brother, of course, because our other two brothers committed suicide. I find it is best between us when that subject is left undiscussed. "You will, of course, come with me," he says, in that formal way of his that nevertheless overflows with warmth. As we leave the vestibule and walk down the hall I see a young student in dirty old pants and a smattered shirt lying on the floor, his back to us, painting the floorboard running along the side of the staircase. I stop, as if to remark on it, or at least to say hello to the boy. "Don't distract him. No. It was his idea, he insisted on doing it, was obsessed with the floorboards." My brother waves his long fingers about and takes my hand, leading me into his kitchen. There is a candelabrum on the gigantic old wooden table that dominates the room and the cupboards are overflowing with inedible looking foodstuffs. It is a kind of Gothic nightmare. And then, as he goes over to his massive sideboard to pour me some wine, I notice that, above it, there are three knives plunged in the wall. I stop and stare at them. I say: "The knives...?" It is a question. He smiles and steps back. "Red or white?" he asks, referring to the wine. My brother loves withholding information, he is nothing if not dramatic. He knows I couldn't care less, I never drink wine. "It doesn't matter," I say. "What about the knives?" "Ah," he says, devilishly, for when he smiles, my brother looks remarkably impish, like a mischievous demon, "you noticed them!" "Of course I noticed them. How could I not notice them? How does one fail to notice three knives in the wall?" He looks at them, with admiration, as he hands me a glass of wine. "They're beautiful, aren't they?" "Well," I have to admit they are, "yes, but why?" "Does there have to be a reason? My logical brother." Now he is just teasing. I know they are there for a purpose if only to stimulate discussion. "I know there is a reason." "Why?" he says, keeping up the game. "Because there's always a reason with you." It's true, meetings with my brother always begin like this, with some extravagant gesture that is followed by an explanation that is more extravagant still. "If you must know, and I see you must." He looks forlornly around him. "I hadn't intended on telling you so quickly. I was saving it for later, but, if you must know, I've been reading Schopenhauer." He says the word Schopenhauer very slowly, theatrically, as if he is raising a red velvet curtain. I frown and take a sip of wine. The wine is delicious, with my brother everything is always delicious, he is a kind of connoisseur. But it is not good that he has been reading Schopenhauer. "Is that wise?" I say. "Surely you, the philosopher, are not going to censor my reading." "I mean, unwise, for you," I say. I see no point in not being frank. "I know the effect Schopenhauer has on you." "Do you?" he says, idiotically. Then, "Cheese? I purchased your very favourite kind of cheese. Are you going to sit down and enjoy it or just stand there and berate me?" I sit because I would like some cheese and I don't approve of the direction of the conversation. I so rarely treat myself. I only eat bland foods. My brother treats himself all the time. I decide there is no avoiding it; if he is going to do his usual breakdown in front of me, which is what the references to me being his only brother and Schopenhauer signal, we might as well get it over with. He goes to the refrigerator and pulls out a massive plate of Camembert. "Do you have something new to say about Schopenhauer?" I ask. He repeats my question. "Do I have something new to say? Do I have something new?" He unveils the cheese and lays it ceremoniously on the table. "Only the best Camembert for my favourite brother." I so wish he would stop saying things like my favourite brother, my only brother. "Yes I have something new to say about Schopenhauer! He is profound and immortal! Immortal and profound." I want to say that he is also bloody depressing, but this will trigger my brother's anger. He's right; just because he has a tendency to be morbid and depressed and suicide runs in our family, doesn't mean that I have a right to tell my brother not to read Schopenhauer. "It's just becoming clear to me, that yes, there is a design. Yes, there is a GRAND design, and we are part of that design, and that design is working through us, and there is nothing, nothing we can do about it." "For example?" I ask. "For example," he answers, "desire." I am caught unawares, this I don't expect, from a brother usually obsessed with metaphysics and who scoffs at psychology. "And what about desire?" I ask. He leans over the table, sipping his wine and sampling the cheese with me. "It works through us, it works inside of us, it works in spite of us, there is nothing that can be done about it. I am convinced that the world has its own plan." "And what is that plan?" "Ah, that's the question, that's the question," he says. "Of course, we will never know." I don't like this craziness. I decide to try and nip it in the bud. "Schopenhauer is mysticism – it's just another way of talking about God." "Is that a bad thing?" he asks, and I see is unwilling to be offended, and on to my trick. "No, it is what it is. It is a religion of Schopenhauer. It is a religion which says that the world works in its own way according to its own plan. I don't happen to think there is a plan. I happen to think that there is only a random order that we can never understand. The only area in which I agree with Schopenhauer is the idea that there is nothing I can do about the way the world works. I am not accusing you of anything, except being a Christian, that's all. Of using Schopenhauer to be a Christian. I don't argue with that, if that's what you want to do. But you should be aware that that's what you are doing." He leans back, casually, eyeing me. "Haven't you ever felt it?" he asks. I don't like it when he does this. I don't like it when he brings my personal life into the conversation. "Felt what?" I ask. "Desire?" he says. I decide it's best not to try and avoid answering him, as he will make me answer him anyway. "Yes," I say. "My brother, the philosopher, has felt desire." He stands up to pour himself some more wine. "Who would have thought that? What was its purpose?" "Its purpose was..." I was thinking of John and of the kiss in the bathroom. I didn't have to answer him. I didn't want to answer my brother. What I really wanted was to turn the conversation back to him. But again I thought it best just to give in somewhat, maybe it would shut him down. I thought that perhaps if he kept drinking, he would forget about me and start ranting, or play the piano. Stranger things had happened. "The purpose of desire is oblivion," I say, thinking very lucidly for once, about my moments with John. "Ah yes! Yes. Yes. YESSSS!" When my brother is excited, he jumps up and down like a child, stamping his feet. "Oblivion yes, desire is a drug! It's all a drug! Its purpose is death! Desire is death! That is the purpose of desire!" "Now you're sounding like Freud" I say, again hoping this will shut him up. My brother, like me, had always detested Freud. "Do you know why you have always disliked Freud so much?" he asks. I shake my head. "Because you are a homosexual." I definitely do not wish to discuss this topic with him, but I don't want to make that too evident. "I don't think it's that simple," I say. "As simple as what – as an explanation of your hatred of Freud?" "I don't like Freud because he claims to be a scientist when he is not," I say. "You don't like Freud," says my brother, "because he's figured it out. He's figured out the death impulse runs through all of us and you don't like the idea that we all want to be dead." I look at him, standing under the three knives, and it seems that the evening is coming to an early end, that it has already reached its climax. "Come with me," he says. "Where are we going?" "Just come with me." He grabs my arm. We start up the back staircase behind the pantry. I know that it leads to his bedroom. I have only been in his bedroom once before. It was not a place that I want to be in again. We hurry up the wooden steps and burst through the door. The room is lying in wait for us, like a restless panting animal. The bed is vast and white and unmade. His white piano, romantically placed under a looming window, is bathed in moonlight. It is like something out of a novel, a play, a dramatic fiction. On top of the piano is a large knife, like one of the ones in the wall in the kitchen, glinting in the moonlight. It is all a bit much for me. My brother moves towards the piano and stands beside it. He pulls a small bag out of the pocket of his jodhpurs. "Would you like a little cocaine?" he asks. He knows I don't want any. I never want any. "No," I say. "Well you won't mind if I have some," he says. I say, "No, I won't mind." I walk over to the wall by the window and stand looking at the piano as he sniffs the white powder. I sit on a chair opposite the piano and notice that on the keyboard he has taped a newspaper article: "Crazed children kill parents in the name of God." I think of asking him why it is there, but then think better of it. "You're sure you won't have any?" he asks. "It really is delicious." I shake my head. He puts the packet back in his pocket and jumps up on the piano seat, standing on it. Then he sits on top of the piano, beside the knife. He pulls up his sleeves. Now I can see why he is wearing a nightshift.

His arms are striated with lines, scabs from where he had cut himself, vertically, with a knife. "What's this?" I say, knowing what it is. "I'm practising," he says. "Practising what?" I ask. "Practising my Schopenhauer." So that's what all this is. It had all been a set-up – the cordiality, the favourite food and wine. Not that my brother doesn't love me, but he loves his own personal drama more. He has planned this little performance as he had planned other performances before. This one was a little more extreme perhaps. Before there had been threats – "I'm going to do something, to do something to myself." "I can't stand it anymore!" That sort of thing. This was taking things one step further. And I knew that it wasn't to hurt me, that it had nothing to do with me, that it was a performance for its own sake, for his own sake, because he was struggling, like we all had to in our family, with what he considered to be the family curse. Looking at him sitting up there, he appeared like something out of an Edgar Allan Poe novel, but a very badly written one. I couldn't just leave him, could I? But I had left The Neurotic. I had left Arthur. The commonplace thought occurred to me – that suicides don't threaten suicide, they just do it – and pleading with him not to kill himself would only play into his narcissistic game. As usual, I should never have come. It felt cruel, more cruel than usual, to leave him like this, but I had done my duty. I had seen him, I had talked with him, I had acted like a brother. Wasn't that why I had come? Or had I just needed a little dose of suicide? Like a homeopathic remedy perhaps I had come for just a little bit of poison. "Excuse me," I said. And I started to walk out the door and down the back stairs. "Where are you going?" he yelled. It really was quite comical. He so wanted an audience for this. Well he would have his student to comfort him. I walked through the kitchen and out the door.

It would be too late for another train. Instead I found a nice hotel, where I am writing this. I should be afraid that my brother might commit suicide. Instead I am quite happy because I am alone. Maybe that's why I came to see him, and it's a very comforting feeling. People are desire, and they are death, as he reminded me. But since death comes anyway, it's more honest to face it by yourself. I thought again, oddly, of Pyotor, who lives beside me in my office in Camden Town, the man who sweeps the road and speaks to strangers, and always desires so much attention. This visit with my brother reminded me that I am not Pyotor; I don't need to be him. It might be time for me to visit Norway again. Alone.

Saturday 3

I stopped in my Cambridge office today, thinking of getting some work done; feeling very focused at last. There was a bouquet of flowers in front of my door. There was a note attached. "I'm sorry for the tea-room. I didn't mean to hurt your feelings. Can we try again?" This was not going to help at all. I sat down at my desk and looked out the window, with the flowers on my lap. What was I to do with him? The answer was surely to let him down easily. Another American film, and I'll tell him that I am planning a trip to Norway – to think and write. And I will explain to him that my feelings were not hurt. That is very important.

Sunday 4

I need an antidote to all this morbidness. With the second visit from The Neurotic, and the visit to my brother, and the flowers from Arthur, I had been inundated with depression, madness and hurt feelings. I wonder how I could have ever thought that a visit to my brother would be a tonic for anything. I spent all Saturday night working on the plans for my sister's house, and I really am quite excited by the work. I don't think they'll understand it; they may even be a little frightened, but I think it's important that I arrange a meeting so that we can talk.

Tuesday 6

Last night I visited my sister. As usual I am of somewhat mixed emotions. But I think I have done the right thing. What I may feel is not important. Certainly the family seems vulnerable to me because they have children involved. But it's important to build a utilitarian thing of beauty, that also, in its own way, defies expectations. A house that resembles life. Upon my arrival all was very much the opposite of what life will be like in the new house. Griselda's husband was reading, safely seated in a Biedermeier rocker of the most excruciating design. The children were playing on a rug featuring a significantly cloying pattern – something involving kittens and pink. As winter was approaching and the nights come earlier, the room was bathed in the warm glow of lamplight. I nearly plunged into a practical architectural discussion, for the atmosphere made me think of one of my principles of illumination, i.e., that lights should either be on or off – at full or in darkness. I would not deny Griselda's family the use of candlelight, of course. A dim little lamplight is only an illusion of the most tasteless kind. Lights should be on for work and off for sleeping. If the family needs warmer gentler light – a light for moments of pure pleasure – let them be frank, and have candles. But I didn't mention any of this, because my sister led me off to the living room immediately upon my arrival. She said she wanted to show me something. She switched on one of the picturesque lamps she had moved onto the table. There were two pieces of paper in her hand. On the papers was an old, formal handwriting, in flowing longhand. "This is something very special," she said. "It is a letter from our grandfather to our mother." Our famous grandfather. He was a legendary figure, at least to us – a German farmer who died in a barn fire when still a young man. He was an alcoholic, that much we knew, and my mother had always implied that his death was a result of his drinking. My sister showed me the signature first. It was signed "From Gretel's Daddy," so it must have been written when my mother was very young. He died when she was still a child. But instead of reading the letter, my sister turned it over and pointed to a postscript. It said, "I haven't drunk anything for some time now and don't intend to, so long as I keep away from it." My sister looked at me in that way she has when we are meant to be sharing an endearing moment. She was thinking of Hermoine. "Does it make you think of anyone?" she asked. Well, it didn't make me think of Hermoine because Hermoine is quite proud of her alcoholism. But I didn't say that. I thought, instead, of my brother's cocaine, and his remarks about desire and death. But I couldn't talk about these things with Griselda. I asked her if I could keep the letter for a while. She said yes, and called to her sweet husband, after telling the children to go to bed. The children were contented and obedient, as always. I wondered what effect their new house would have on them. I looked at Griselda and the country doctor, gazing at me with such trust, and it occurred to me that today's discussion might be unpleasant. I explained to them, very carefully, the principle behind the children's rooms. Each room, I said, will be a challenge to the child. One of the girls is a little dreamer, always planning and chattering and excited about the future. She is sure to encounter obstacles to her idealism. So I created a kind of maze leading to her room. The room itself would feature windows too high to look out of, and barriers everywhere – a barrier around the bed, a barrier in front of her bathroom – so that the theme of a maze might continue from the hallway into the room. It was a little bit like a nightmare, as any life might turn out to be. The other little girl is the opposite of her sister, somewhat of an intellectual, always reading, quiet, eager to do her homework, absorbed in her studies. I imagined that someday the real world would make an unwanted intrusion on her life. Thus, the walls in her room could be made to completely disappear, so that she might be surrounded by the outside world. There would be no curtains, only walls that would slide away to reveal floor-to-ceiling windows. Since the site we had chosen was in the middle of the woods, there would not be any issues of privacy. She would have two choices, to live in a windowless room or to be surrounded by an overwhelming outside world. Because I considered her to be very much like myself, I designed a room that would most resemble my experience of society and solitude. Their response, when I revealed the design for the two little girls' rooms, was very unlike that at our first meeting. They hid their feelings more efficiently. Both wore placid smiles, urging me to go on, occasionally saying "interesting, how interesting…fascinating" and the like. Finally we arrived at the little boy. He is quite typically a little boy, and the youngest, always running and jumping. For him I designed a truly singular space; I wished to create significant physical challenges for him. For instance, the floor of the room would be on a gentle slope, just enough to make it odd and difficult for him to walk about. And if he tried to run, he would perhaps hurt himself. I know this sounds cruel, but children are resilient, especially little boys, and they bounce back. The walls would be built in such a way that they would gently slope away from the floor, meaning that they would always be out of his reach and give him the feeling that he could never really touch them – that they were always moving away. Of the ceiling, I was particularly proud. I was able, through a complicated feat of engineering, to make it appear as if it was going to fall on him at the centre. All of this would inhibit his young movements, as the world soon would, and anticipate what would soon be his experiences of life's difficulties. I talked for a long while, because I described not only the rooms but also the philosophical implications of them. I wanted to make sure that the couple completely understood the design. I was quite prepared for rejection. I know that the designs were extreme. There was a long pause, and they looked at each other, as if they had prearranged what they were going to say. Then my sister looked at me and said – "Now I hope you won't take this the wrong way, but it almost seems as if you want to build the house this way…in order to torture the children." I knew she didn't want to hurt my feelings, and on the contrary I was pleased with her acuity, frankness and perception. "That is precisely correct," I said, "because life is torture, to some degree, and this house will help them to deal with the future." My sister smiled and held her husband's hand. "What do you think, dear?" she asked. "Whatever you think, darling," he said. She turned back to me. "We're very, very excited about our new house, and can't wait to start building it," she said. I was again, amazed by their reaction. It occurred to me that I have perhaps long underestimated the foresight and open-mindedness of the bourgeoisie. Their reaction gave me hope – not just for the future of their children – but the future of the world in general. We had some coffee afterwards and they talked about the children's development, their trials and tribulations at school, etc., as they often do. Then we said goodbye. I told them I would work on the final plans and take them to an architect to begin the tedious process of drafting to my specifications.

Wednesday 7

It happened relatively quickly. That is the essence of this kind of change. I credit Arthur with a good deal of it. Indeed, I credit Arthur with all of it. I have a newfound respect for Arthur. It even goes beyond respect. I see now so clearly that I have been feeling, all too frequently, when I should have been thinking. Ironically, it has been a thought which has turned me around, has turned me upside down, or inside out; turned me against thinking. Like a Möbius strip; my inside is out and vice versa. Gertrude Stein is reported to have said about Texas that "there is no there, there." I now think not that there is no 'there' there, but that 'there' is somewhere else. And I speak in terms of life. This must be set down clearly, because, despite how profound my new thoughts seem, a mere feeling may wash it all away. After all, it is a thought *about* feeling. Yes, we went to a third film. Arthur noticed that *Going Hollywood* was playing again, and remembered from my lecture that I was fond of the film. He was apologetic, he was discouraged by our failure to enjoy previous films together, so he invited me with him to one that he knew I would enjoy. I could see no harm in this. My original plan was to use this opportunity to tell him that this would be our last encounter, that there would be no future movies together. I noticed that he was more attentive than usual, more concerned about my well-being. He asked, for instance, if I wanted to sit in the balcony again. He may have been afraid that duplicating our location might duplicate the negative experience from before. I told him it didn't matter. So we did. This time the theatre was nearly filled. My taste is obviously the common taste, and also there is a great affection these days in England for the films of Marion Davies. From the very start of the movie, things were different between us. I don't know if Arthur planned it that way. I noticed that my arm happened to graze his arm. In previous instances, he had pulled his arm away. This time he did not. It was bizarre; but I didn't think much of it. I expected that he, as usual, would be moved to tears, romanticize the leading lady, etc., while I would be left all alone to analyze it, trying in vain to make him understand. This was not to be. First of all, I was carried away by the film even more so than on my first viewing. I found Marion Davies to be a completely believable and sympathetic heroine, with the kind of feminine American pluck that is so appealing. At the beginning of the film she is trapped in her boring job teaching. No situation could be more real to me. Of her antics to persuade Bing Crosby to love her – well I thought nothing could be more endearing. And the final fantasy sequence – *Make Hay While the Sun Shines* – held me more firmly in its thrall than ever before. It was a kind of ecstasy, as the daisies swayed in time to the music and Marion Davies watched herself dancing. What was most moving to me was the relatively simple moment – simple but not commonplace – when Bing Crosby first sings at the microphone. Marion Davies joins hands with him, and suddenly they are strolling through a field of daisies. This moment thrilled me for no reason at all. It was all the more exciting because it was merely a fancy, a conceit, based on the idea that one can be in one place and then suddenly find oneself somewhere else. And so vividly brought to life! When the film ended, I sat hypnotized, unable to move. This is what I expect a good film to do: leave me helpless and confused. I think that's what we all want, what we all dream of, to be vanquished in this manner. Such a state is frightening but enormously exalting too. Arthur tapped me on the hand, I shook myself to life. Feeling embarrassed about the effect that the film had on me, I tried to restore a semblance of my usual self. I suggested we go back to the tearoom, but Arthur would have none of it. As it was a pleasant night, I agreed to walk. It was windy enough to remind me of Cornwall, but my brother's craziness was the furthest thing from my mind. It was one of those very crisp evenings on the very cusp of winter. Then we began wandering. This is unusual for me, I usually want to know exactly where I am going, but uncharacteristically I let Arthur take the lead. In fact I don't know where we actually went. I don't remember and I don't care. I only know where we ended up. Arthur wanted to know what I thought about the movie, whether I liked it as much, seeing it for a second time. I told him that I enjoyed it even more. He seemed pleased by this; in fact it had been his only wish that I enjoy it. He asked, "Why did you like it so much more than *Bringing Up Baby*?" since both films presented irrational, skewed realities. I told him that this one was much more skewed; there was no reason in it, only rhyme. Arthur asked me to tell him my favourite moment. I said – when Marion Davies leads Bing Crosby out of the recording studio and they find themselves in a field of dancing daisies. "And why this moment?" he asked. I told him it was an impossible moment, that it could never happen in real life, that it confounds reason, that a recording studio is a recording studio. He said, "I must contradict you there." This was bold of him. I have never known a student of mine – even a graduate student – to contradict me. We turned and stopped. We were beneath an old archway underneath a very large building. The archway was crumbling and made of stone. I did not know how we had gotten there or even precisely where we were. I had never been there before. I knew where we were, from looking around, but I wasn't at all sure where 'there' was. "I don't think that moment in the movie was impossible," he said. "Certainly it was," I said, about to deliver a short lecture on Aristotle. Then Arthur did a very odd thing. He suddenly put his finger on my lips to quiet me. No one had ever done this to me before. It struck me that he must have had something very important to say. And then Arthur said, "Don't you understand how a recording studio can suddenly became a field of daisies? It is because they are in love. And when you fall in love, you enter another reality." And it seemed to me, at that moment, that this was a very interesting idea indeed. But before I had time to think about it, I found myself acting in an uncharacteristic manner. It must have had to do with the fact that I did not know where I was, and therefore perceived myself to be alone. I do not mean alone in the sense of being apart from people, I mean alone in the sense of being apart from my thoughts. I had no thoughts. I had only feeling. I remember feeling that he looked very handsome in his shabby suit; and that it was shabby because it was too short, revealing his inappropriate white socks, and because he had never fixed the pocket, and because the collar was frayed. I remember feeling that there was something very beautiful about the fuzz on his cheek and the contrast that it made with his lush lips and his reddened cheeks. I remember feeling that all I wanted to do at that moment was kiss him. I did. The moment or two after that I don't remember anything. This is a good thing. I should not like to remember everything; I cannot analyze that moment because I don't know what happened after I kissed him. But soon after, we were walking again, somewhere. And it was a field – and though there were no daisies – it reminded me of the field in the film. And ever since that moment my mind has been seized with the idea of another reality which exists alongside this one. It is an idea related to Einstein, but it is also an idea which is not rational. And that paradoxically is what I like about it – the fact that this idea defies reason. It is an idea about what it is like not to have an idea; what it is like to feel. For when people allow themselves to feel in this way, they cross over into another reality, and they are able to see things that they once saw in one way, in another way completely. It suddenly became evident to me that Arthur was a very fine young man, worthy of my attention and respect. And that he was, also, a very lovely young man. Worthy of my love. No, he was not Antony, would never be Antony – but that was the very point of it all. And no, he was not John, would never be John, and thank God for that. Appealing as John is, I don't think I could be with John for more than the time it took to *wrassle* with him. All at once, in that moment, Arthur became what I now think he really is, someone who is worthy of my respect, and perhaps, it seems to me, of my love. If you ask me why this happened, I cannot explain it. And that is the strange beauty of it all. I had stepped over into another land. Where I had stepped to, it would be impossible for me exactly to tell you. But I know that I am there now. Or I am not. Or perhaps both here and there at the same time. Or perhaps I am nowhere. A chilling but oddly exhilarating thought.

Thursday 8

As long as it stands, this new way of being is an interesting experiment. It causes me to wonder what the repercussions might be in my relationships with people who are not Arthur. In my office today, I had a visitor who went a long way towards helping me to answer this question – The Neurotic. I had thought I was done with him, I had thought that I had sent him on his way forever, armed with the comforting cliché that his mission in life was to 'smell the flowers'. But his ruminative, tortuous, self-critical malcontent would not rest. It's as if pain and endless self-analysis were a giant hand that had his brain in a vise grip, squeezing it to a pulp like a helpless, melancholy grapefruit. A knock on the door and there he was: purple gloves and orange scarf. Only now his eyes were red from crying and rimmed with black from lack of sleep. I actually felt myself feeling sorry for him. He plunked himself down opposite me and said, in a strange, muted, slightly strangulated voice, "I'm sorry to bother you, but I didn't know what to do." It struck me that the game he had been playing with melodramatic language and ever expanding self-deprecation had reached its perilous climax. I hoped it would not be too late. "I am obsessed with you," he said. "I know there is no reason to be. I don't even know you. But I can't get you out of my head. Your successes, your intelligence, your books, your achievements, every aspect of your life! You are in my head. And you are killing me there! Of course it's not your fault, but I constantly compare myself to you. And

I am in every way lacking. I can't work. I can't think. I don't know what to do. Can you help me? Please?" Gazing at this poor, tormented creature the solution was immediately clear. "There is only one thing to do," I said. "What?" he asked. It occurred to me that if I had told him to kill himself he might very well have done so. "I am not here," I said. "I don't understand," he said. "I do not exist," I said. "What are you talking about?" "I'm telling you that I don't exist." "But I'm sitting here looking at you," he said. "Not if you decide that I am not." "But how can you say that? Of course you are here. Are you not a professor of mathematics?" he asked, astutely, I thought, for the first time. Already he was beginning to come closer to real life. "I am a professor of logic," I said. "But how can you – as a professor of logic, say that you don't exist?" "I am telling you," I said, "with all the authority of a professor of logic, that I am not here." "Who says?" he asked cunningly. "You do." "I do?" he asked. "Yes," I said. "It is up to you. I want you to think for a moment of what your life would have been if you had never met me, never heard of me." I paused for a moment to let him think. "Wouldn't it have been better?" "Yes," he said, "it would have been so, so much better." "So travel there. Go to that world. I can tell you that you have clearly decided to live in a world where my daily existence tortures your innermost being. Well, you could just as easily be living in a world where I am not there." "But you do exist," he said. "Not if you don't think about me. It will get to the point that if you see my name in print you'll simply ignore it. We don't process information that we don't think it is important to worry about. For instance, you know that right now a man called Hitler is about to invade Poland. How can we continue to live happily when we hear this? Yet still, we do nothing. We hear of that atrocity and put it out of our heads. Or perhaps you would like to stop worrying about me, and start worrying about Poland? Poland is more worthy of your thoughts than I am, is it not?" My example was heartless, but thankfully, efficacious. The Neurotic stood up, proud of himself; a changed man. "Of course. Why should I think about Poland? My life can go on without thinking of Poland." "Of course," I said, "Millions of people go about their daily lives not thinking of Poland. Most of them don't think of me either. It's completely up to you. Me? Poland? Something else? Which reality do you chose?" He rushed over to me from the opposite side of the desk. I could tell he was going to either embrace me or shake my hand. He did both. "Thank you, thank you he said. How will I ever repay you?" "By not thinking of me." I said. "Yes, yes I will," he said, almost dazed, but very happy. "I will not...think of you ever again." He stood in the doorway. "I won't say good-bye, because you're not here." He turned and marched down the hall. I pondered putting up a shingle. I could be the new Freud! If only I didn't detest him.

Friday 9

Another day; another opportunity to test my new arena, the mysterious location of my consciousness. Nigel appeared in the doorway of my office. He mentioned that he had lately seen The Neurotic strolling about, looking healthier and happier. He knew of him because I had previously gossiped about the situation. Nigel loves joking about the students, especially the undergraduate infants; in fact it is his favourite pastime. Their inadequacies especially fascinate him; their ineptness at love. "At that age they are all in love, for five minutes at a time!" is one of his favourite sayings. I was surprised to see him, but also invigorated by the opportunity to experiment with my new situation and the effect it might have on our relationship. "Well I'm sorry to keep pestering you," he said, "but I am still concerned about your position on cognitive relativity." I could not understand why he would be concerned about such a thing. Why could he not hold his own opinion and I mine? I was certain that we would never agree, and why should we? But I could not stop him; since he had not been offended by my previous rather serious rebuke, it would be necessary for us to have it out. He came into my office and sat down. "Would you mean to suggest, by cognitive relativity, that we would not understand what our ancestors were saying, and would have no possibility of accessing it?" He had been thinking, I would give him that. "Yes," I said. "Absolutely." "But how can that be true?" he asked. I had had enough of this. "Look," I said, "it is extremely misleading for us to talk about what is true and what is not. What I refer to is a fundamental challenge to all that is true and false, real or not real. What I am suggesting resolves a contradiction which has long plagued me. For since all of us in England in 1938 speak the same language, we should therefore have the same experience of reality. But I am not certain that we do. This can be accounted for by slight differences in perception, i.e., some people are blind, some can only see certain colours, etc. But it is more than that. I am convinced that there are fundamental cognitive differences between civilizations, over time, and between different languages, and actually, sometimes, between people. There are other worlds. We do not know them because we could not perceive them. It happens that we pass over into another world, it is often by chance. All we can do is wonder that we are there. It is as if – if I may be so bold – as if we were to say that this office at Cambridge is not merely an office at Cambridge, but in fact it is a field of dancing daisies. If I perceive it to be a field of dancing daisies, I have stepped over into another reality and that is now where I am. The field of dancing daisies perhaps exists – as do the people who live among the daisies, simultaneously, along with this more familiar world that we think we know. But we are hampered from seeing it, for whatever reason. Of course we cannot challenge the existence of this other world, because the only way to know it is to experience it, and when you are experiencing it you have moved into another realm of cognition and cannot experience your old one." "But what you are describing is irrational," he said. "Yes," I said, triumphantly. "Exactly." "But you are a logician." "Exactly," I said. "But is that not a contradiction? How can logic describe something that is not logical?" "That is exactly my point. I, the logician, am describing something which it is impossible to describe through logic. In fact I would hope that no one ever tries to explore it that way. This is not something for the men in white coats." "Or perhaps," he tittered "it is – for the little men in white coats who might want to take you away." I accepted his jibe; he was feeling insecure, and the joke eased his discomfort. "May I ask you what brought you to this startling conclusion?" he asked. "You may," I said, "but I don't know if I will answer. "Well, what was it?" "I will tell you if you promise not to tell anyone," I said. "I promise," he said. I thought yes, you promise; in another reality I might believe your promise, but in this reality you are lying. However, I couldn't resist. I really didn't care who he told. I leaned over and whispered: "It was love." "Love? he asked. "Yes, love," I said. I could see he was holding back his typical disgust and scepticism. I don't know if Nigel has ever experienced love. I do know that he very much loves his Pomeranian. I now believe that his love for that animal is a very good thing indeed.

Saturday 10

It has happened. I was working in my office in Camden Town and received an urgent phone call – no one is allowed to call me there but certain people have my number – from my sister Griselda. It was about Hermoine. She was dying. It was after midnight so I hailed a cab which took me to her address. In the hallway her old lady's maid was seated in a chair by the door, crying. My brother let me in. He was dutiful, repentant, in black formal wear, as if it were the funeral already, and not the moment of expiration. He said, quietly, "You should go in there now." I understood and walked back towards her bedroom. When these things happen, they happen so quickly. And you don't want to miss death. The door was slightly ajar and I could hear moaning and my sister Griselda's voice. Her husband the doctor was standing beside the door on the opposite side of the bed. He immediately came over to me – "What is happening?" I whispered, just beginning to take in the drama of the scene. "It's happening," he said. "I have helped her...she is feeling no pain." The picture on the bed was operatic indeed. My sister was sitting on the side of bed, leaning over, her hand on Hermoine's chest. Hermoine was propped up against her fluffy pillows. She looked as if she had already died, was a sepulchre, white as the sheets themselves, her mouth open, gasping for air. Griselda was chanting the same words, over and over, her other hand caressing Hermoine's arm, "Yes," she said. "Yes, it's alright, Hermoine, you can go now, you have our permission to go, yes, it's all right with us, please, yes go, feel free to go, yes, it's all right, yes, please go." This litany of final release went on for some time. I did not want to interrupt it. It did not seem entirely appropriate, in my opinion. I assumed that Hermoine had expressed some insecurities about leaving us to remain in this world without her. But I did not think this was probable, mainly because it would have been so unlike Hermoine to express that kind of sentiment. At any rate Griselda was not to be interrupted, certainly not by me. Finally her husband edged over to her and proffered, "Griselda... Griselda..." very quietly, "your brother is here." Griselda immediately let go of Hermoine, who lay back on the pillows, her mouth open, and her eyes closed, but as I could see, she was still breathing. Griselda was full of warmth and condescension, as if the whole world had become a small child. "I'm so happy you're here!" she said. "Hermoine would love to talk to you, to say good-bye!" This did not seem possible. The sight of death was not at all new, nor was it surprising to me. I had seen death many times on the battlefield, in the hospital. I had seen deaths in agony and those under drugs. But I was not as familiar with the state in between. I had also not been close to any of those men who I saw dying. The prospect of saying good-bye to Hermoine made me very uncomfortable. She never acknowledged the fact that she was going to die, or even the fact that she was ill. She had treated her illness as one of life's vicissitudes, one that had to be borne all in the name of living beautifully to the very end. But this end was not beautiful. Of course I could not refuse Griselda's request. "Come along...come along," she said. I followed her and she placed me on the bed beside Hermoine. She sat on the opposite side. Then, in a slightly louder but gentle voice, she whispered, "Hermoine,

Hermoine..." and gently rubbed Hermoine's hand. Hermoine's eyes opened. Her sockets were hollow and her eyes bulged widely. She looked at us. "Oh you're here, you're all here...and Henrik?" she asked. "He's just outside the door," said Griselda. "Then we're all here." She looked over at me. "Ludwig," she said, gently, fondly. She was trying to smile, which was in stark contrast to her bulbous eyes. "Ludwig...you found time in your busy schedule at the university...to come visit me?" "Of course I did," I said. I didn't know what to say. "Oh that's nice," she said. I was not entirely clear if she is being sarcastic, but of course at this point it didn't matter. I was at a loss for what to say, so I was horribly thankful when her eyes began to close and she leaned back on the pillow again. "Yes, you're all here. That's good. You're all here," she murmured. I was startled by this concern. Of course the woman was dying, but she had never expressed concern that we come to visit her, and always seemed surprised when we did. I was pleased to see that she seemed as contented as she might be, but wondered how much this might have to do with the pills that the kind doctor had given her. But that is what she wanted, wasn't it? She had been longing for oblivion – courting it – and now she had it in spades. That is a dreadful thing to write. But how could I not resent her for not taking care of herself? However, this was not a time for recrimination. It was a time to simply be there, if needed. Griselda leaned over her sister again and began the keening chant. I did not know whether Hermoine could hear her, Griselda was obviously convinced that she did. I wished Griselda would stop that infernal noise. I stood watching, again, quite moved and frightened by the picture of one sister calling the other to her death. But Griselda waved me away, and her husband took my arm, and I was ushered out of the room. The maid was still crying, only more softly now, and my brother was pacing near a large curtained window opposite the stairs. When he heard me come in he stopped and turned. "It's Schopenhauer," he said shyly. "It's that damn will, doing its work." Then he looked down again sheepishly. Well, it didn't matter to me how apologetic he was about his thoughts. He might as well have said to me, "God works in mysterious ways." In fact he had said it, in an atheistic manner. I wanted to hit him. But instead, I only thought about pitiful humanity trying so desperately to force a pattern on what is ultimately ceaseless random disorder. Death, particularly, because it is so unpopular, offers an opportunity for proselytizing. Is death not supposed to teach us something? Well, it should teach us to stop wondering about the meaning of death. Finally the good doctor appeared at the door. "She has passed," he said quietly. My brother looked at me, then looked at the floor, and walked towards my sister's door. I followed.

Monday 12

There must be a funeral. And there was. It turned into a bit of a comedy. This is not a bad thing; I am not at all certain that Hermoine would have disliked that, would even have desired a wake. She had made no mention of how she wanted to be remembered, and since she had spent so many of her last years in bed retreating from life, we had quite forgotten to wonder. Griselda thought it necessary to have a Catholic service. I found this unbearable, but thankfully it was a tiny church and relatively newly built, so the service was not the least bit moving. It annoys me to be accidentally moved by a religious ceremony. Oscar Wilde used to go on about the wonders of Catholic service; it was in this case not only paradoxical but also idiotic of him. The priest was a small man, and it was a small room, a tiny chapel at the back of a tiny church. He did not know Hermoine of course, so what could he say? Only what he was expected to. What I had hoped for, longed for really, was a gaggle of Hermoine's past suitors. I had hoped especially to see The Count, the most esteemed of all her admirers. He was not there. There was only the immediate family and her maid, and a few tradespeople whom she had known and dealt with from her bed in her final days. It was no use looking for The Count – after all, he was probably older than her and quite dead now. Did he even exist? Did it matter? He brought her so much pleasure, in her memories, that it seemed a moot point whether he actually existed or not. Arthur was at my side. He would have had it no other way, was very concerned, which touched me. He seemed somewhat disappointed that I was not closer to my sister. When I described her to him, he said, "She sounds like Greta Garbo," which was like him. I told him that she most decidedly was not. Or she was an earthbound Garbo, which is even less pleasing than that mad actress could ever be. And then, about halfway through the service, when I was not listening to the words (for how could I?) and trying not to be carried off by the music (for there is a poison in that too), a strange thing happened. A girl entered, dressed in black and an ugly hat, at the back of the chapel. She tried to be unobtrusive but it was impossible with so small a crowd and so boring a priest. Arthur and I had a clear view of her because we were off to one side, and she and her escort walked along the back of the chapel and up the other side. I recognized her as the girl who "came in, to clean" during Hermoine's last years. What makes such tradespeople come to a funeral? Perhaps she found something to love in that old lady who coughed so theatrically upon her weekly visits. But the sight of her escort made me do a somersault, inside. I tried not to jump on the outside. It was John. So this must have been his newest chippie. I was consumed with the worry that he might recognize me. The new reality I had been living in, the new hotel that I had checked in to – ever since kissing Arthur under the archway – was suddenly in peril. I looked over at Arthur, who didn't seem to notice the panic I was experiencing. I realized that there was no need for him to ever know. John was unlikely to openly flirt with me at a funeral. But on the other hand that was not my real worry. The real worry was that I would want to do something with John again. Not at the funeral of course – at *any* time. I had conveniently forgotten about John, the physical reality of John, and here he was taunting me, trying to pull me out of the new place where I was so comfortable, in love with Arthur. Would I have to choose? For there was a part of me that couldn't imagine not *wrassling* with John ever again. I was very uncomfortable about this for a minute or two. And then it occurred to me to stop thinking about it. Yes, to stop thinking. It had worked for the Neurotic, it had worked for me under the archway, it had worked with John many times. It might work again. Yes, it was possible that something might happen again between John and me. But John was not Arthur and Arthur was not John. And I could not see the sense of trying to position myself in a specific place in relation to one or the other. Perhaps there was a point equidistant between them like the vertices of a polyhedron. A significant idea occurred to me, at that moment – oddly for the first time. John cannot read. It suddenly seemed very significant to me that he was functionally illiterate. When the service was over, we retired to a lovely vestibule, much more beautiful than the chapel, had cakes and tea, and tried to remember the very best of Hermoine. I found myself not thinking of Hermoine, but of the horrible house that I designed for Griselda and her family. No. That would not do. I could not let them live in that torture chamber. My conception had been rigorous but mean spirited. I could finally see that. I whispered this to Griselda, and she hugged me gratefully. Would she ever have let me build it for her? I fear she would. When I turned around after talking to her and returned to Arthur, John caught my eye from the other side of the room. He winked at me, as if to say, "We're still on, aren't we mate?" I couldn't resist. I winked back. It was not a mistake. It was simply that for a moment I had forgotten again where I was.